PURRFECT STAR

THE MYSTERIES OF MAX 70

NIC SAINT

PURRFECT STAR

The Mysteries of Max 70

Copyright © 2023 by Nic Saint

Edited by Chereese Graves

www.nicsaint.com

Give feedback on the book at: info@nicsaint.com

facebook.com/nicsaintauthor
@nicsaintauthor

First Edition

Printed in the U.S.A

PURRFECT STAR

The Spy Who Killed Me

They say that all good things come in threes, but also that misfortunes never come singly, so I'll let you decide which of these proverbs applies to the following situation: first we discovered that a thief had been stealing our litter, thereby preventing us from doing our business the way we like to do it. And then one of our country's most beloved actors was found murdered aboard his private yacht, with plenty of suspects likely to have done the deed. And if that wasn't enough, Gran and Scarlett decided to reform the Neighborhood Watch Committee and actively insert themselves into the investigation, wreaking havoc and mayhem at every turn. In other words: troubled times lay ahead in Hampton Cove, that peaceful little town on the East Coast that always seems to teeter on the verge of disaster.

PROLOGUE

*J*ane Collins was walking along the quay and gazing out at the pretty boats and yachts that were moored in the Hampton Cove marina. It was a nice change of pace from being cooped up inside her home, where she had been hunched over her latest sewing pattern design. As a fashion designer, Jane had made quite a name for herself on sites like Etsy, selling her patterns to a great number of happy customers.

She wouldn't have minded boarding one of these yachts now, she thought as she looked upon their owners and passengers with a certain measure of envy. What she wouldn't give to be far away from Hampton Cove and to lie on deck, her hand trailing in the warm azure waters of some tropical paradise, cloud gazing and generally letting the world go by. It would certainly be a nice change of pace from what she was used to. As a mother of four, she knew what responsibility was, and had been taking care of her offspring and her husband Bert for so long now that she often forgot that she also existed and also had a right to lead an exciting, wonderful and fulfilling life. Not that her patterns didn't give

1

her a certain measure of satisfaction, and she certainly had received plenty of acclaim. Only not from the people who really mattered to her.

Which was why she was now walking along the marina and wondering about the choices she'd made. If she hadn't married Bert, for instance, but decided to somehow hang on to the other man in her life—in many respects the only man she had ever loved. She hadn't seen Robert in years, which hadn't stopped her from wondering if her life would have been different if they had stayed together. The man had certainly done very well for himself. So much so that he was being presented with an award by the Hampton Cove Chamber of Commerce. Ever since she had heard the news that her ex-boyfriend would be in town, she had felt unusually restless and wondered if she shouldn't leave town while he was there, almost as if she wanted to avoid him. On the other hand, she wanted nothing more than to clap eyes on the man who had broken her heart twenty-five years ago.

She paused for a moment in front of a particularly huge yacht that lay at anchor. Called the Aurora, she was sleek and gorgeous, and as Jane stood admiring her graceful lines, suddenly a person emerged on deck who looked vaguely familiar. But as she looked closer, she realized it was none other than Robert himself. He looked older, of course, but still as handsome as ever. He must have recognized her, too, for he did a double take, then slowly removed his sunglasses as he took her in. For a moment, the two ex-lovers simply stared at each other, then Jane saw that a single tear glistened in the man's eye, which is when she decided that maybe second chances existed after all, and she set her foot onto the gangway and stepped aboard.

CHAPTER 1

*D*ooley had been snoring softly and was generally lost to the world when a strange sound made him prick up his ears and immediately return to full wakefulness. The sound seemed to come from somewhere nearby, and even though his first thought was that Max had produced the sound, upon further inspection he discovered that his friend was still sleeping peacefully by his side and hadn't moved an inch since they had fallen asleep together on the couch.

Dooley now lifted his head to take in the rest of the living room, turning his ears like antennae to scan his surroundings for a bead on the source of the sound, but try as he might, his ultra-sensitive ears could not pick up the sound again. Almost as if its design had been to bring him out of his peaceful slumber and then down tools, knowing its work was done and nothing more was required.

He yawned and stretched and decided to have a bite to eat, take a trip to his litter box, and generally do what cats do when they wake up and before they go right back to sleep. It wasn't too much to say that today was a day like most other days, with the marked difference that he didn't think the sun had been out in such splendor in quite a while. Hampton Cove had been blessed with plenty of rain lately, but now nature had apparently decided that enough was enough and had turned off the tap, bathing the world in a sunny glow for the first time in about a week. Nature was celebrating, for the birds were tweeting up a storm outside, the bushes and trees in the backyard all looked green and lush, and even the lawn looked as if it was in urgent need of a trim.

As he walked to the kitchen to see if his bowls were still filled to his satisfaction, Dooley noticed that the pet flap was gently swinging, as if someone had recently passed through there and had quickly left again when they became aware of his presence. He didn't pay any mind to the strange phenomenon, figuring it was probably either Brutus or Harriet, the other two cats in their household. In due course he reached his bowls, and saw they still contained sufficient amounts of the good stuff, then made a beeline for his litter box for a tinkle. And that's when things turned a little weird. For when he arrived there, he saw that all the litter was gone, and not just in his personal litter box but also in Max's!

For a moment he simply stared at his empty box, scratching his head in wonder. That someone would have entered the house through the pet door to steal food from his bowl or drink his water was something he could have wrapped his head around, but why would anyone decide to steal his litter? As far as he knew, litter wasn't one of the major food groups. It wasn't nutritious, and possibly might even be harmful when ingested. And as he sat staring at his empty litter box, the front door of the house opened and closed, and moments later Odelia entered the kitchen, Grace on her arm, and he shared with her the gist of his complaint. Namely, that as a healthy grown-up kitty, he wasn't merely in regular need of sustenance but also of a receptacle to deposit the end result of his mastication and digestive processes.

Odelia, who clearly was as surprised as he was, promised she would look into the matter post-haste. At which point she simply walked out of the kitchen and left Dooley to his own devices, making him wonder if maybe he had failed to impress upon her the urgency of his request. Then again, he now realized she had looked a little distracted. In fact, she had only listened to him in a sort of half-hearted way and looked upon him as only a human could: her eyes seeing him, her ears hearing him, but her mind a million miles away. Almost as if she was dealing with problems of her own. Which was impossible, of course, for what could be more important than a sneak thief who went around stealing litter from innocent cats?

Shaking his head at such a lack of cooperation, he decided to return to the couch and pour his lament into Max's ears. Max would listen. Max would understand what was going on here, and most importantly, Max would act and fix things. Max always did. Dooley didn't know how, but his friend was one of the great fixers in the world. Anything that was wrong, anything that went missing, any person or persons engaged in some form of wrongdoing, Max managed to right those wrongs and generally make things fine again. It was his greatest quality and what had made him Hampton Cove's very own feline Sherlock Holmes. And the great benefit of being friends with such a powerhouse of detection was that Dooley had access to that formidable brain at all times, which was both a blessing and a curse. A curse in the sense that a lot of people lay claim to Max's time, often causing Dooley's problems to take a back seat, just as they now had with Odelia. But also a blessing, for often Max only needed a single word to know how to proceed. But as he now approached the couch with the intention of uttering just this single word to place his friend in possession of the facts pertaining to the strange case of the missing litter, he saw that of his friend... there was not a single trace!

Somehow, in the five minutes that Dooley had been gone, Max had skedaddled. This made Dooley realize that the worst had happened—the thing he had feared the most for the longest time. Along with his litter, this mysterious sneak thief had also... stolen Max!

CHAPTER 2

*O*delia wasn't feeling at the top of her game. Not only did she have several articles to finish and multiple looming deadlines hanging over her head like the proverbial swords of Damocles, but the woman who ran the daycare Grace attended had sent a message in the parents' WhatsApp group stating that due to a family emergency, the daycare would be closed for the next couple of days. This meant alternative solutions had to be found. Consequently, Odelia had paid scant attention to Dooley's litter lament and had immediately rushed out the door in search of her grandmother, hoping she would find the old lady next door.

She found Gran gazing intently at a caterpillar that had taken up position underneath a leaf on one of her precious rose bushes, seemingly transfixed on the bug. Observing the intensity with which her grandmother regarded the caterpillar, Odelia thought she wanted to zap it with her eyes, laserbeam it into oblivion. When Odelia cleared her throat to alert her of her presence, Gran redirected her gaze and, for a moment, something stirred within Odelia as she experienced the full impact of the old lady's baleful eye. But then Gran's

7

gaze softened, and she even managed a smile. She probably had realized that Odelia was not a caterpillar.

"I've been keeping an eye on that one," she announced. "The old Vesta would have killed it dead, but the new Vesta wants to protect life. It's all about the preservation of life, you see. If we want to save the planet from destruction, we need to do it one caterpillar at a time."

"So you're going to let it eat your plants?" Odelia asked, surprised by this position.

"I didn't say I'm going to stand idly by and watch it destroy my lovely garden," Gran replied. "I said I'm keeping an eye on the little bugger. And if I see it take so much as one bite out of this here rose bush of mine, I'm going to pounce." She wagged a bony finger at the caterpillar. "Consider this your first warning, buster! One bite and you're out. Is that clear?"

"Gran, could you babysit Grace for me? Chantal at the daycare sent a message saying she's dealing with a family emergency and she has to close the daycare for the next couple of days."

"Oh, sure, honey," her grandmother said vaguely, her attention still riveted on the caterpillar, indicating she wasn't paying much attention elsewhere.

"Could you do it now?" asked Odelia. "I'm already late for work. I didn't see Chantal's message until I arrived at the daycare with Grace." She hadn't been the only one either. Three other moms had also arrived, surprised to find the daycare closed for the day, with a sign on the door informing them of Chantal's unexpected unavailability. It was highly unusual since Chantal Jones was a most conscientious and dedicated daycare owner, who loved the kids in her care as if they were her own. For her to suddenly close up shop was disconcerting, and when Odelia had more time to spare, she would definitely pay her a visit and see what was going on.

She sincerely hoped Chantal wouldn't be inconvenienced indefinitely. Otherwise she'd have to find a different daycare, which might prove to be a tough proposition, as most of them were already full and didn't accept any new charges, especially a couple dozen of them.

"Sure, sure," said Gran with a wave of the hand. "Just leave it with me."

She would have pointed out that her daughter was not an 'it' but a 'she,' but then she knew it would be pointless. Once Gran had her mind set on something, it was pretty much impossible to shift it. So she placed Grace on the porch swing, kissed the top of her head, and hurried off again. Not only did she have several articles to write, but she also had an interview scheduled with the one and only Robert Ross, the multimillionaire actor whose yacht had arrived in the Hampton Cove marina just the other day and had attracted so much attention.

Robert Ross was a local man who had left his home town many years ago to try his hand at different endeavors. According to local lore, he had worked as a handyman in a maharajah's harem, had competed in several boat races alongside the Prince of Brunei, and had even been the personal bodyguard of the Crown Prince of Jordan. He earned the man's eternal gratitude when he saved his life from an assassination attempt. During that particular act of heroism, he had sustained a gunshot wound to the stomach, which had been successfully remedied with the first pig-to-human stomach transplant in history, earning him an entry in the Guinness Book of Records.

After his checkered career, he had been selected as the next James Fox, and had now finished no less than six very successful Fox movies in a row, becoming one of the most popular actors ever to play that famous British spy. In other words, the man was a legend. When the rumor spread that his yacht was arriving in the marina, all of Hampton Cove showed up to greet him and give him a hero's welcome. Even Mayor Butterwick and Odelia's uncle had been there, although the latter's presence was for professional reasons only, to prevent anyone from trespassing or assaulting Mr. Ross aboard his vessel.

She hopped into her pickup and raced away, although the behavior of her aged Ford pickup was more akin to rattling away, as the noise the car made could probably be heard three streets over. She really should get a new one, but when she had asked Dan if he couldn't by any chance provide her with a company car, the editor had chuckled amusedly, pointing out that the newspaper trade was a dying industry and she was lucky to still have a job. Perks like company cars were not in the cards, unfortunately, and would never be as long as she insisted on working as a reporter, as opposed to, say, an investment banker or a stock broker.

She arrived at the marina in due course and parked her car between a Porsche Cayenne and a Tesla, doing her best not to scratch either. She knew that these wealthy yacht owners didn't take kindly to scratches on their precious cars' paintwork. She hurried across the boardwalk to the quay where all the fancy yachts were moored. It didn't take her long to spot the Aurora, Robert Ross's personal yacht. It was easily the largest one in the small harbor. Recently, the marina had been completely redesigned and now featured a few luxury boutiques and fancy restaurants catering to the yacht owners who liked to visit these shops before heading into town. A more rustic experience awaited them there. If it were up to Charlene Butterwick, she would probably redesign all of Hampton Cove. However, she would face opposition from the locals, most of whom preferred things the way they were and had always been. Not that Odelia could blame them. Hampton Cove was a pretty pleasant town, even though it appeared a little sleepy to the more hip and cool segment of the tourist class.

She stepped onto the gangway to board the vessel, hoping Mr. Ross wouldn't be too upset that she was running late. But when she arrived on board, she was surprised to find that the yacht seemed to be deserted. Normally, for a man of Mr. Ross's stature, she had expected to encounter a small regiment of security personnel, personal assistants, and other crew members. However, she had boarded the vessel without being stopped, causing her forehead to wrinkle up in a frown. Having been on yachts before, she had some understanding of how they operated. Therefore, she headed to the bridge first, hoping to find a sign of life. The door was, of course, locked, which was understandable. As she walked along the deck, lightly placing her hand on the bulwark, she traversed the vessel from bow to stern. To her disappointment, she found no trace of the famous movie actor.

She had reached the stern of the yacht and gazed up at the upper deck, where she knew a Jacuzzi and a small pool were located from the pictures she had seen. But there was still no sign of the boat's current resident. That's when she decided to climb the small metal ladder leading to the upper decks, hoping to find the actor sunbathing on the top deck, possibly having fallen asleep and forgotten all about their meeting. As she rounded the corner, she laid eyes on the small pool, a gorgeous azure blue in contrast to the beige wood of the deck, and noticed something floating in it. Moving closer, she saw that it was a person's body. Without a moment's hesitation, she jumped into the pool, swam with a couple of powerful strokes of her arms to reach the person, and started dragging the lifeless body back to the side of the pool.

Moments later, with a supreme effort, she hoisted the body out of the water and placed it face up on the decking. It was Robert Ross, and he appeared very much dead.

CHAPTER 3

When Dooley started messing about in the kitchen, and then Odelia walked in with Grace on her arm, I decided to desert my pleasant spot on the couch and go in search of more peaceful pastures to continue my nap in an uninterrupted fashion. I don't know about you, but I enjoy consuming my naps in one long session. So, I relocated to the rose bushes at the bottom of the garden, hoping to find them uninhabited by our housemates Brutus and Harriet, who often like to spend time there, engaged in their lovey-dovey activities.

I was in luck, as I found the location free of any lovers, whether pet or otherwise, and with a sigh of relish, I settled down for the long haul. Or at least that was my intention. It soon became clear to me that it simply was not to be. Above me, an insect that looked vaguely familiar drew my attention to its plight, and before long, it was talking a mile a minute.

"Yo, Max," said the creature, which at this point I had positively identified as a caterpillar, "I've got a problem that's been giving me a headache."

I had the impression that the caterpillar was about to

transfer this headache to me if I didn't get to take my nap, but nevertheless, I asked, "What is it?"

"Well, I've been hounded by this huge monstrous beast that seems intent on eating me, for some reason I can't possibly fathom."

"What beast, and why does it want to eat you?" I asked as I marveled at the mass of feet this creature had. I wondered how it never got them entangled. I guess there must be some kind of system in place.

"I'm not sure," said the caterpillar. "Oh, my name is Joe, by the way."

"Max," I said, "but then I guess you already knew that."

"Of course!" said Joe. "Who doesn't know the great Max? So the thing is, I've been hanging out here and minding my own business, when all of a sudden, this huge... thing homes in on me. Sometimes it's carrying a can and threatens to 'zap me to kingdom come.' Other times it tries to grab me and says it will 'turn me to mush.' Now, is that nice, Max? Is that kind? No, it sure ain't. So, I would like you to go and talk to this monster and tell it to lay off already. As far as I can tell, I never did anything to upset the beast, and still, it keeps hounding me!"

"What does this beast look like?" I asked.

"Like a scarecrow," said Joe, "but uglier."

"Okay, so an ugly scarecrow."

"Exactly. And it's not just me this scarecrow keeps harassing. It's been happening to all of my friends too. It just goes around threatening us with destruction, and for what? Just because we happen to be alive? That's no way to treat any creature, Max, and it's definitely not the way I like to be treated."

"You wouldn't happen to have a name for this scarecrow, would you, Joe?"

The caterpillar thought for a moment, then finally nodded. "I think I've heard it being referred to as... Pesto?"

"Pesto."

"Yeah, must be a nickname." Suddenly, the caterpillar glanced up, and a look of alarm came over his tiny face. "Don't look now, but there it is. There, the monster comes!"

Ignoring Joe's strict instructions, I did look up and saw that Gran had approached the rose bush and was peering at it intently. She did have a can of some kind in her hand, I now saw, and I understood what was going on.

"Gran, don't use that bug spray on me," I told her immediately.

"Oh, Max," said the aged relative. "I didn't see you there for a moment. You wouldn't have seen any caterpillars, would you? It's just that my backyard has been invaded by the species, and they're eating all the leaves and destroying my precious plants and flowers."

Joe, who had taken to hiding underneath a leaf, now made frantic gestures in my direction to attract my attention. "Don't tell Pesto where I am!" he whispered loudly.

I shook my head as a sign that I wouldn't, causing his features to relax.

"No, I haven't seen any caterpillars," I lied to Gran. "But why are you trying to destroy them? You do know that eventually caterpillars become butterflies, right? And that they're a boon to any garden, a source of infinite pleasure with their colorful displays and graceful flights and flutterings."

"I don't care about any flutterings," said Gran, a bit more harshly than I would have liked. "All I care about is the survival of my flowers, and with all these voracious bugs hanging around, that won't be happening."

I eyed the can of bug spray with a curious eye. "I thought you were against the use of bug spray?"

She eyed the can with a look of wonder. "Oh, will you look at that? Who put that there?"

Gran had been going on about ethical gardening a lot lately, which as far as I could make out meant that she wasn't going to use any chemicals when she tilled her modest little patch with her claw rake, carefully removing weeds and making the soil ready to give of its best.

"Chemicals destroy everything and turn the earth into one big garbage dump. Isn't that what you said, Gran?" I asked.

"Of course, of course," she said. "Which is why I don't understand what this is doing here," she added, then proceeded to throw the can as far away from her as she could. It sailed across the hedge dividing our backyard from the next. There was a sort of loud thunking sound, followed by a soft yelp of pain, and moments later, Tex Poole, Gran's son-in-law, appeared in the opening in the hedge, rubbing his head and looking understandably irate.

"What's the big idea!" he cried. "Pelting me with cans!"

"That wasn't me," said Gran, even though she was the only one present.

"Of course it was you! Don't think I haven't seen you secretly using that spray on my flowers."

"Those are my flowers, and there's nothing secret about it. I was simply trying to get rid of those caterpillars."

"So you admit that you threw the can," said Tex.

"I will admit to no such thing!" said Gran, tilting her chin a little higher in a posture of indignation. "It was Max!" she said, pointing an accusing finger at me.

"A likely story," Tex scoffed. "Max couldn't throw a piece of kibble, let alone a can."

I would have told the doctor that I can indeed throw a mean piece of kibble, but since my opinion clearly wasn't required, I kept my tongue. Instead, I lay down again,

15

watching the proceedings like one of those spectators at the US Open. I had a feeling this might prove extremely entertaining. I was even willing to postpone my precious nap to take it all in.

"Not only have you been using these horrible chemicals on my flowers, thereby poisoning the soil and endangering every species on the planet, but you threw that darn thing at my head!"

"That was an accident," said Gran quickly. "Max probably thought he was doing us a favor, but in his haste to get rid of the can, he failed to take into consideration that a certain person or even persons might find themselves in the flight plan of said can."

"You threw that can," said Tex, directing an accusatory finger at his mother-in-law. "Besides, why is it so important to get rid of those caterpillars? They're a very beneficial species, and besides, they turn into butterflies. You wouldn't murder a nice, innocent butterfly, would you?"

"Of course not, are you crazy? I would never raise a hand in anger at any creature, great or small. You know this, Tex. You know that I'm essentially a peaceable person and abhor violence of any kind." Tex actually rolled his eyes at this, and it wasn't that he was about to experience a fainting spell, but more to express his reservations about Gran's statement.

"Whatever," he said finally with a throwaway gesture of his hand. "But I'm confiscating this," he said, holding up the can. "And I better not see any more of this poison in my backyard."

"It's my backyard, too!" Gran cried indignantly.

But Tex had already left to return to his own backyard—having lost a few of his illusions but gained a tiny little bump on the head.

"That man drives me crazy," Gran grunted as she resumed

her search for any trespassing caterpillars. "He always thinks he's right, even though half the time he's not."

"Shouldn't you both be at the doctor's office?" I asked. "Or have all of your patients been cured?"

"We're taking a day off," said Gran. When she saw I was staring at her with a sort of puzzled look on my face, she said, "Even doctors can take a day off, you know. It's hard work having to treat all of those patients, so from time to time, we need to take a break and not see any patients for an indefinite period of time."

"How long are you and Tex going to be out of commission?"

"Like I said, for an indefinite period of time."

"Is that your definite answer?"

She smiled. "Smart-ass."

CHAPTER 4

I don't mind caterpillars or my humans taking the day off, or even half a day, but what I do mind is if all of this hullabaloo prevents me from doing what I consider my most sacred duty as a feline: taking long, extended naps. After all, my humans often like to consult me on minor and major mysteries that have left them baffled. But what they don't understand is that for a brain to work at full capacity, plenty of rest is needed. So, I decided once again to relocate, this time to the house next door, where I hoped I wouldn't be disturbed.

And I was traipsing along when I was arrested by a loud yell or scream.

"Max! You're alive!"

I turned back to see that my friend Dooley had uttered these immortal words.

"Yeah, last time I checked, I was still alive," I said in response.

"But... I thought you'd been grabbed by the litter monster!"

Now I've heard of the cookie monster, of course, but this

was the first time the term 'litter monster' was used in my presence. For a moment, I wondered if I should take the bait or not. Doing so might lead us off on some tangent that most probably would eat into my nap time. But then my natural curiosity asserted itself. "Who or what is the litter monster?"

"The monster that ate our litter," Dooley explained, making his meaning not all that clear. "And abducted you." He gave me a keen look. "Have you been abducted, Max?"

"No, Dooley. I escaped from the house under my own steam."

He visibly relaxed. "Oh, phew. For a moment there, I thought you were dead."

"I almost was," I admitted. "If Gran had used her bug spray on me, I might not have survived the ordeal. But as luck would have it, I caught her just in time, saving both myself and Joe in the process."

"Who is Joe?"

"The caterpillar whose life I saved," I explained and gestured to the rose bush where Gran was still giving Joe the evil eye, even though by all rights she should be keeping an eye on Grace instead. "I was just going next door," I told my friend. "Seeing as it's too busy out there, and I can't seem to get any shut-eye. Wanna join me?"

"Absolutely," he said. "Now that Odelia's house is being targeted by the litter monster, we need to get away before it attacks us next!"

I would have rolled my eyes at this, but since my eyelids were growing heavier by the second, I didn't. Instead, we ventured into Marge and Tex's house, and moments later, we found ourselves staring into Brutus and Harriet's litter boxes, which oddly enough, were both empty!

"Oh, no!" said Dooley. "It's the same monster. It must have been here too!"

"That's impossible," I said, even though the facts were

19

clear. Both litter boxes were devoid of litter, having been neatly cleared out. In fact, whoever had done the job had been so meticulous there wasn't a single piece of litter left. Almost as if they had been cleaned out with wet wipes.

"It's probably Gran," I now suggested. "She must have decided to clean out our litter boxes and then forgot to refill them." Gran walked into the kitchen, looking like a woman on a mission. So when we posed the question, she seemed annoyed. "Not now," she barked. "I've got a hot date with a caterpillar."

"A hot date with a caterpillar?" asked Dooley. "But Gran, isn't that... weird?"

She stared at him for a moment, then shook her head. "It's not a *date* date, Dooley. And it's only hot for him, not me." Her lips twisted into a vicious grin. "In fact, it isn't too much to say it will be very hot. Very hot indeed." With these words, she grabbed a lighter from one of the kitchen drawers.

"But Gran!" said Dooley. "You can't set fire to a nice cater-pillar! Don't you know they turn into beautiful butterflies?"

She grumbled something under her breath, looking caught, and quickly dumped the lighter back into the drawer. "So I just let them destroy all of my plants, is that it?"

"I'll talk to Joe," I assured her. "I'll tell him to take his busi-ness elsewhere and leave our plants alone."

Gran gave me a look of such devotion I felt a little tingle travel up my spine. She had clasped her hands together as if in prayer. "You would do that for me, Max?"

"Of course. Now, about this litter business."

"What litter business?" she asked, the look of devotion quickly being replaced by one of annoyance.

"You cleaned out our litter boxes," I said. "But forgot to refill them."

"I did not clean out your..." She crouched down to look

into one of the two boxes and now frowned. "Well, I'll be damned. Tex! Tex, come here a minute, will you?"

The kitchen door opened and Tex walked in. Like before, he was dressed in his gardening outfit, which, in his case, consisted of a pair of old jeans and an even older sweater with holes in them. "Now what?" he asked.

"Did you clean out the cats' litter boxes and then forget to refill them?"

He stared at her. "Of course not. That's your job, Ma." Even though we have lived with Tex for many years, he still considers us 'Marge's cats' or, conversely, 'Odelia's cats' or even 'Vesta's cats.' Maybe he has a point, since we also consider these ladies our humans, with Tex and Chase their appendages. Like spin-offs from the main feature. And it is true that Tex never feeds us or takes care of our litter boxes. He did install our pet doors, which is something, I suppose. And he tolerates us, which is very kind of him.

"So, who cleaned these litter boxes?" asked Gran.

"Marge, probably," said Tex. "Or Odelia. And now, can I go back to my tomatoes?"

As an experiment, Tex has been trying to grow his own vegetables. Ever since the prices of common household items and foodstuffs have risen precipitously, our humans decided to put the small plots of land they possess to good use and try to yield a modest harvest. To that end, Tex had planted several seeds and was hoping for a good crop when the time came. He's also been thinking about raising chickens for their eggs, but so far, Marge has put her foot down and is refusing to budge. I guess she feels four cats are enough denizens of the animal kingdom to contend with and doesn't want to add a dozen chickens to the mix.

The good doctor had left the kitchen, and Gran, hoping to get to the bottom of this minor mystery, now put her phone to her ear and called her daughter. But when Marge told her that she hadn't touched our litter that morning and had no idea who had, the mystery only deepened. Which is why when Gran's phone rang next and she picked up, she barked, "Odelia, did you clean out the cats' litter boxes this morning? No? Then who the hell did!" She listened for a moment, then redirected her gaze to us. I could see that whatever Odelia was telling her, clearly concerned us. And to confirm this, she said, "Yeah, I'll tell them. Right now? The marina? Yeah, okay. So do you need me? Uh-huh. Uh-huh. Uh-huh."

Dooley looked at me, I looked at him, and I think we both had the same expression of curiosity written all over our faces.

"Uh-huh, uh-huh, uh-huh," said Gran, not really giving us a lot to go on.

"What's with all this 'uh-huh,' Max?" asked Dooley.

"It's an expression of confirmation," I said. "Instead of saying 'I understand' or 'I see,' people simply say 'uh-huh.' Like a sort of shorthand."

"Gran's hands are short," he confirmed, taking in the elderly woman's hands. "But I still don't see why she can't use her words, like any grown-up."

Grace had toddled in through the door and now stood stock-still, taking us in. She did that sometimes, and it often made me wonder what went through her head at moments like these. Possibly she saw dead people, like that kid in the Bruce Willis movie, and listened to what they were telling her. She now redirected her attention to us. "So is it true what they're saying?"

"What are they saying?" I asked. "And who are they?"

"Well, Brutus and Harriet, of course. They're saying that you and Dooley have been using their litter boxes, and they were so dirty that Marge had to clean them ahead of time, and now they have nowhere to do their business except in Blake's Field, so they did."

And as if to prove she wasn't kidding, Brutus and Harriet now walked in through the door. "Max!" Brutus growled, taking a menacing stance in front of us. "You did your business in my litter box, didn't you? And now it's empty."

"It's the litter monster," Dooley explained. "It's been eating our litter."

Brutus frowned at my friend. "What are you talking about, Dooley?"

"Oh, can't you see what's going on?" asked Harriet. "He's simply protecting Max."

"Protecting Max?" asked Dooley. "From what?" But then his eyes went wide. "Oh no, it's the litter monster, isn't it? He's eaten our litter, and now he's coming for us next!"

"Don't talk nonsense, Dooley," said Harriet in a snappish way. "Everyone knows that there's no such thing as a litter monster."

"There is! There definitely is! And it's eaten all of our litter!"

Brutus and Harriet shared a look of surprise. "I don't get it," Brutus finally admitted as he plopped himself down on his tush. "Start from the beginning, will you, and omit no detail, however slight."

But before Dooley could do just that, Grace decided to step in. "Someone or something is eating your litter," she explained. "And that someone or something just might still be in the house!" At this, she glanced around in a meaningful fashion, causing the hair at the back of my neck to stand at attention. We all gave the kitchen a look filled with trepidation and downright fear.

"The litter monster is still here?" asked Dooley in a shaky voice. "Are you sure?"

"Where else could it be?" asked Grace. "First, it ate all of your litter, Dooley, and Max's, and then it polished off Brutus and Harriet's litter, and now it's taking a nap. Just like me when I've eaten too much."

"But, but, but..."

"Oh nonsense," said Harriet. "There's no such thing as a litter monster. Max simply couldn't hold it in, and so instead of running home to his own litter box, he decided to do his business in mine. And then, since Dooley always has to do whatever Max does, he did the same thing in Brutus's box. And when Marge got up this morning and found our boxes unusually soiled, she decided to clean them out, and then since she was busy with a million other things, like humans always are, she completely forgot about it."

"I've been going to Blake's Field," Brutus lamented. "And I think I sat on a nettle. My tush is itching."

"You should lick it," Harriet advised. "Lick it until it stops itching."

"But I don't want to lick my tush!" said Brutus. "What am I, a dog?" He glanced up at Gran, who was still engrossed in her phone conversation, seeking her urgent assistance, but the old lady ignored us. So he now asked Grace, "Could you do the honors?"

"What honors? What are you talking about?" asked the little girl.

"Clean my tush? Normally, Marge always does it, or Odelia, or even Gran. But since they're all otherwise engaged..."

Now it was Grace's turn to roll her eyes. "Oh, all right. But just this once, you hear?"

"Marge always uses antibacterial scented wet wipes," Brutus explained. "They make my tush smell like lavender. It's very nice."

"Yeah, they've got aloe vera," Harriet added. "It helps

soothe irritated skin and greatly reduces the presence of blemishes and wrinkles. It's also hypoallergenic."

"God, you guys are spoiled," said Grace as she climbed a chair to reach the box of wet wipes located on the kitchen table. Moments later, she was applying a wet wipe to Brutus's tush, much to the latter's enjoyment. And since he looked so thoroughly satisfied, the rest of us stood in line for the treatment, waiting patiently until Grace had finished with him so she could apply those wonderful wet wipes to our tushies as well. "And to think that *I'm* the baby here," she grumbled, "and that *I'm* supposed to be the one who gets her tushy wiped."

Even though her hand-eye coordination might not be up to snuff yet, and she had a hard time focusing on the job at hand, ending up wiping half of my belly in the process, she still did a pretty good job, and besides, it's the thought that counts. At the end of the process, the box of wet wipes was empty, and we had never smelled more like lavender before.

So when Gran finally ended her phone call and saw the floor littered with used wet wipes and the four of us looking happy as clams, she shook her head. "I won't ask what happened," she said. Then she turned to us. "Odelia needs you out by the marina."

"Oh no," said Dooley. "Not another boat trip!"

"No boat trip," said Gran. "Another murder!"

CHAPTER 5

*W*hen we arrived at the marina, traveling in Marge's little red Peugeot driven at breakneck speed by Gran, the place was already crawling with police cars. Gran had a hard time getting past the cordon, but fortunately, that wasn't a problem we faced. So we simply passed through the police officer's legs and hurried to the scene of the crime. It took us a slight moment of hesitation to traverse the gangway, as the plank that connects a ship with the mainland is called, but then we were on the boat, in search of our human.

We found Odelia and Chase on the top deck, which surprisingly enough housed an actual pool, and we saw that the victim had already been removed from the pool and placed on a stretcher. The man looked very much dead, I have to admit, which is probably normal when you've just been murdered by a proficient killer who knows what they're doing.

"So, what's going on?" I asked when we had toddled up to Odelia. She was seated with Chase and a third individual who was wearing a captain's cap, causing me to guess that he was, in fact, the captain of the vessel. The man looked thoroughly shocked and couldn't drag his eyes away from the victim.

Odelia would have given us the lowdown on what was going on, but obviously, she couldn't, so she merely gestured with her eyes at the pool. Catching her drift, I wandered over to inspect said pool and see if I couldn't detect any clues that she or the crime scene people might have missed.

The pool was a smallish affair, which probably is normal since it was located on a boat, where space is mostly at a premium. As we walked around the pool, there was nothing out of the ordinary that I could see until we suddenly stumbled upon a smallish creature of the canine persuasion, seated on a lounger and giving us a keen look of alarm. The happy little yapper did not seem pleased to see us, and now I understood why Odelia had asked us to head this way. She wanted us to interview the dog while she interviewed the captain. A nice example of teamwork in action.

"A dog, Max," Dooley whispered as he also spotted the creature.

"I can see that it's a dog, Dooley," I said.

"I'll go talk to him," said Brutus. "I'm not afraid of a little dog."

"Oh, but I'm not afraid either," I said. "Just careful, you know."

"And you should be careful, tootsie roll," said Harriet, referring to her boyfriend, not me, with this quaint epithet. "Dogs can be mean, especially the small ones, and they have a nasty bite."

"He won't bite me," said Brutus. "You have to fix them with one look, you see. That's the trick. You have to show them that you're not scared and that, in fact, you're the alpha male. Obviously, Max can't do that since he's a wuss, and

Dooley can't do that either since he's basically a soft-bellied little pussy. And..." He eyed his girlfriend uncertainly.

"Yes?" said Harriet with a touch of ice in her voice. "What am I?"

"Well, you're a girl," said Brutus finally, picking his words carefully.

"And you're a dinosaur," said Harriet acerbically.

Dooley laughed at this. "But Harriet, Brutus can't be a dinosaur."

"And yet, he is," said Harriet, then stepped to the fore. "I'll talk to the dog. You guys wait here."

And so she approached the dog, and we watched as she did. And even though I had fully expected her to be attacked by the creature, or at the very least receive the cold-shoulder treatment, instead, cat and dog seemed to get along well, and before long, they were chatting amiably. Which I have to say rankled to some extent since I'm supposed to be the detective, interviewing witnesses and possible suspects, only now Harriet was doing my job for me.

Brutus must have seen I wasn't happy with the state of affairs, for he grinned at me. "Don't like being sidelined by a girl, do you, Maxie baby?"

"No, I don't," I said. "And for your information, it has nothing to do with the fact that Harriet is a girl. I just don't like to be kept in the dark, and if this dog saw what happened, then..."

Harriet rejoined us, a satisfied smile on her face. "Flame says she didn't see what happened, for one of the crew members was walking her when Robert fell in, but she does feel very sad about his demise."

"Robert? Not Robert Ross?" I said and directed another, closer look at the victim, who was still being examined by Abe Cornwall, our county coroner. And as I looked, I saw to my surprise that Harriet was right. The victim was indeed the famous James Fox actor, who had played the spy six times in a row to much acclaim, from the public but also from the critics.

"Who's Flame?" asked Dooley.

"The dog," Harriet pointed out.

"What a funny name," said Dooley as he regarded the dog with interest.

"It's because of the color of her fur," said Brutus. And the dog did indeed look as if she had recently been set alight, her fur being an odd blend of red and streaks of beige. She was of the Papillon variety and was still eyeing us in an alert sort of way, clearly not all that happy with the presence of four cats trespassing on her territory.

"So she wasn't hostile to you?" I asked, much surprised.

"Oh, no, absolutely not," said Harriet. "I told her we're police cats, you see, and she said she's only too glad to help since she can't possibly imagine who would want to harm her human, who was the most wonderful and amazing man on the entire planet as far as she was concerned."

"Did she say anything else?"

"Nothing of note, Max," said Harriet. "She was out walking with a member of her human's crew, so she didn't see anything. When she left, Robert was still alive and getting ready for a swim, and when she returned, Odelia was here and Robert was in the state he is in now."

"Odelia found him?" I asked.

Harriet nodded. "Looks like. At first, the crew member thought that Odelia had harmed the man, but when she produced her credentials, she understood. Apparently, Robert had set up an interview with Odelia but wanted to have a refreshing swim before she arrived."

"So was it murder or an accident?" asked Dooley.

Harriet shrugged. "Odelia said it was murder, and the dog doesn't know."

There was a sort of commotion on the staircase leading to the upper deck, and moments later, Gran's head cleared the edge. She didn't look happy. "They tried to stop me!" she said. "Can you believe these people? The Chief's mother!"

Behind her, a police officer had also appeared, her face red, and her eyes burning holes in Gran's back.

"You can't be here, Mrs. Muffin," she said. "This is a crime scene."

"I'm your boss's mom," the old lady pointed out. "If I wanted to, I could have you fired like that!" She snapped her fingers.

"That may be so," said the woman, "but you can't be here, so I have to ask you to leave. If you don't comply, I have no choice but to place you under arrest."

"Oh, you wouldn't dare."

"I most certainly would."

For a moment, the young policewoman and the old lady squared off, but then Chase approached. "It's fine," he said.

"But, sir."

"It's all right, Sarah."

And with a final dirty look at Gran, the woman retreated to prevent other rubberneckers and lookie-loos from crashing the crime scene.

"You have to hand it to her, she's feisty," said Brutus.

"Feisty and tenacious," I said.

For a moment, Gran bent over the body of the dead actor, then shook her head. "So sad," she murmured. "I thought he was pretty great as Indiana Jones."

"James Fox, Gran," I pointed out. "Not Indiana Jones."

"Oh?" said Gran, though she didn't look all that interested in exactly what role the iconic actor had played. "So how did he die?" she asked Abe Cornwall.

Abe gave her a scrutinizing look, then said, "I didn't know you had joined the force, Vesta."

"I haven't, but as a concerned citizen, it's my sacred duty to get involved in the investigation. After all, where would we be if we allowed these murderous individuals to run riot in our town?"

"That's why we have a police force," Abe pointed out, but the corners of his lips had curled up in amusement.

"Look, I gave birth to a policeman," Gran pointed out, "which gives me all the knowledge I need to handle cases like these. So how did he die?"

Abe sighed. "Well, I'm not sure yet," he admitted. "He doesn't appear to have any water in his lungs, which tells me he was dead before he hit the water."

"Heart attack?" asked Gran. "He wasn't in great shape, was he?"

Abe frowned. "He was one of the finest specimens of the male species I've ever seen, Vesta. Muscular, well-toned. Obviously, a man who took great care of himself and worked out on a regular basis. Though even so, a heart attack is always a possibility, of course." But then he seemed to realize he was basically discussing a case with a member of the public, even if she had given birth to the chief of police, and clammed up. "The rest you'll have to ask your son, I'm afraid." He had gotten up from his position next to the body and now walked over to Chase to confer with him about his preliminary conclusions.

"Hmm," said Gran as she fingered her chin. "If Odelia says it's murder, she must have her reasons, even if Abe doesn't want to disclose them. So let's just say the man was shot—"

"No gunshot wounds," I said.

"—stabbed."

"No stab wounds."

"—garroted?"

"No—"

"All right, all right, smarty-pants. Then how did he die?"

31

Against my better judgment, I had approached the dead man and now sniffed. I detected a powerful smell of bitter almonds and nodded knowingly.

"Poisoned," I concluded, therefore. "Mr. Ross was poisoned with cyanide."

CHAPTER 6

*O*delia hoped that her cats would be able to get something out of that dog. Since it belonged to the dead man, the dog must have a vested interest in seeing its owner's killer caught. Or at least she hoped it would. In a recent investigation, they had encountered a dog who had been glad that her humans had been murdered. Though that was admittedly a very peculiar case.

She refocused her attention on the captain.

"Yeah, like I said, Robert loved being pampered. He couldn't even pour himself a drink and expected to be waited on hand and foot day and night. So when he told me that he needed the crew to leave the vessel so he could be alone, that set off all kinds of alarm bells in my head. But since he was the boss, we did as we were told and got off board."

"Did he tell you that he had scheduled an interview with Odelia?" asked Chase.

The captain shook his head. "He never shared that kind of information with me, I'm afraid. The guy was pretty much an enigma. Didn't talk about himself and kept a distance from myself and my crew. He was a major movie star, of course, and guys like Robert often are that way. Friendly but distant. But I have to say that Robert took it to the extreme."

"How do you mean?" asked Odelia.

"Well, we weren't supposed to look him in the eye for one thing, and we had to avoid bumping into him as much as possible. Preferably, he would have liked that we served him in as unobtrusive a way as possible. Invisible, as he called it. He wanted to feel as if he was the only person on board, or if he was traveling with friends, as if they were alone on the vessel."

"Tough proposition," said Chase sympathetically.

"Oh, but he's not the only one," said the captain. "Yachts in this price range are often chartered by the rich and famous, and mostly they hate to come into contact with the crew, whom they often deem unworthy or beneath them. As if we belong to a lower class of people."

"So where did you come from now?" asked Odelia.

"We spent a couple of months in the Bahamas and the Caribbean before we arrived here."

"Did he have a shoot there?"

"No, just vacationing. We've been slowly making our way up along the coast."

"And there was no one else on board except Mr. Ross?"

"That's right."

"We'll still have to talk to the rest of your crew," said Odelia. "I hope you understand."

"Of course. And you're saying he was murdered?"

Odelia nodded. "That's what the coroner seems to think."

It had come as a huge shock when she saw the man floating in the pool, and then when she tried to revive him, she had quickly determined that it was no use. The paramedics had arrived very quickly, followed by police officers who had cordoned off the marina, and when Chase arrived he had immediately taken the investigation in hand, as he always did, with admirable fortitude and professionalism. Slowly the crew had trickled in, as apparently they had been given the morning off so Robert could be alone. What she didn't understand was why he would want to be alone with her. She had never met the man, and it wasn't as if she was a big celebrity herself, just a reporter from a small-town local paper. But from the way Captain Gerard said it, Robert had made it out as if he was meeting someone very important and absolutely did not want to be disturbed as he did. Surely that person could not be her?

Her cats now approached, and Max told her that Flame, apparently Robert's dog's name, said she had been taken for a walk when her human had died and couldn't help them identify her human's murderer any more than the captain or the rest of the crew could.

Which made her wonder who this mystery person that Robert was meeting could be. She now posed the question, but Captain Gerard shook his head.

"Like I said, he never divulged that kind of information to us."

"But he must have told you who was coming if they were going to eat on board," said Chase. "Or if they were going to stay for a couple of days."

"He had a habit of springing surprises on us," said the captain. "But then still expecting a five-star service for himself and his surprise guests, which made us have to jump through hoops to make the impossible possible, like sourcing the most elusive dishes out of thin air. One time when we were traveling from one port to another, he suddenly said he had a craving for apple sauce. But since we didn't have any apple sauce stocked, or any apples we could puree, he demanded that a helicopter be chartered to get the apple sauce and land on the helicopter deck. And then he didn't even eat it." He shook his head. "Such a waste."

"Sounds like you weren't a big fan?" asked Chase.

"I was, until I met the guy," he said with a grimace.

"Never meet your heroes, huh?"

"You can say that again."

CHAPTER 7

*G*ran may have managed to insert herself into the investigation, but that didn't mean she would prove to be a boon and not a hindrance. Judging from the dark looks Chase kept darting in our direction, I had the impression that he wasn't fully on board with the concept of Gran joining in the hunt for Mr. Ross's killer. He may have allowed her to stick around, but that was more out of deference to the Chief and not because he thought she was a great detective. Before long, Gran was traveling along the deck, her eyes glued to the floor, hunting for clues and generally making a spectacle of herself.

Finally, Odelia felt she needed to intervene and came ambling over. Her interview with the captain having terminated, she had decided to take matters into her own hands.

"Gran, why don't you go home," she told her grandmother. "I'm very grateful that you gave the cats a lift, but I think we can take it from here." Then she seemed to think of something else. "Wait, if you're here, then who is looking after Grace?"

"Oh, you've got nothing to worry about," said Gran. "Tex is babysitting."

"Dad? But doesn't he have to work?"

"We took the day off," said Gran simply, causing Odelia's eyebrows to shoot up into her fringe. "Even doctors have a right to take a day off, you know," she said, reiterating the same sentiment she had shared with us at the house. "Now what are we looking at here? A possible murder? Max says he smells cyanide on the guy's breath?"

"Robert Ross is dead, Gran," said Odelia. "So as a rule, he's not breathing anymore."

"Whatever."

"Did you say he was poisoned with cyanide?"

"I didn't say it, Max did. He says he can smell it on the guy's breath."

Odelia glanced down at me, but short of looking like a fool, she refrained from engaging me in conversation. So instead, I confirmed that I had indeed smelled cyanide on the man, and that possibly he was poisoned.

"So what do you want me to do?" asked Gran.

"I want you to go home," said Odelia emphatically.

"But I want to help! I am the mother of a police chief, you know, so I know a thing or two about police work."

Odelia had to smile at this. "All right. Why don't you put your ear to the ground in town and ask people what they've heard about Mr. Ross. And also try to find out if he's been ashore recently and any people he met in town." She frowned. "Captain Gerard just told us that Robert Ross asked the crew to leave the ship so he could be alone. He thinks he was probably meeting someone, but since Ross never talked about his private affairs with a member of the crew or even the captain himself, he has no idea who this person could have been."

"Could it have been you?" asked Gran. "You had an appointment for an interview."

"I very much doubt it. I had never met the guy, so he had no idea who I was. And besides, the captain says he wanted the ship emptied out before ten, which means he was probably meeting his mystery guest at that time. My interview wasn't scheduled until noon, which would have given him plenty of time to meet his person and then see them off again."

"What time did he die?"

"According to Abe, between ten and twelve, though probably closer to ten."

"When his guest arrived. So whoever this guest was, they probably killed him."

"That's why it's imperative that we find out who this person could have been." She placed a hand on her grandmother's shoulder. "And why it is so important that you talk to people in town."

"Count on me, Odelia," said Gran warmly. "Though to do this properly, I'm going to need a couple of assistants."

"What assistants?" said Odelia. I had the impression she was simply trying to get rid of her grandmother in a graceful way.

"You've got Max and Dooley. Let me have Harriet and Brutus, and I'm your girl."

Odelia smiled. "Fine. You can take Brutus and Harriet, and I'll take Max and Dooley."

"Deal," said Gran, and the two women shook hands on it.

"And that's how we're sold down the river for thirty pieces of silver," said Harriet dramatically.

Gran and her 'assistants' left the scene stage left, and Dooley and I, feeling happy with the promotion we had received, followed Odelia as she and Chase began the long slog of interviewing the other crew members. The interviews took place in the mess, located next to the galley, as the kitchen on a ship is called, and where the crew members ate their meals.

It didn't take long before a pattern started to emerge. Robert Ross, as Odelia told us between two interviews, might have been a man who hated to interact with the crew of his luxury yacht, demanding that they didn't look him in the eye and remain 'invisible' at all times, but that didn't stop him from hitting on young female members of that same crew and trying to get them to supply certain extracurricular services. For a man of his stature, this surprised me a great deal, as he probably could have been with any woman he wanted. Still, he seemed to have a certain predilection for the youthful female crew members. And it was as Chase and Odelia were interviewing one such person that they stumbled upon something both ominous and interesting.

The crew member in question was a young woman in her early twenties with long blond hair and quite a striking beauty. Among other things, she had been responsible for serving Mr. Ross his meals, a task she said she hadn't always pulled off without a hitch.

"Robert Ross hit on you? But I thought he wanted the crew to be invisible?" asked Odelia.

"Mostly, yes, but apparently that rule didn't apply to me," said the girl with a grimace. Her name was Suzanne Palmer, and she seemed extremely nervous as she kept chewing her nails, her eyes darting all over the place, as if looking for an escape route. "He even asked me to join him in his suite a couple of times, and when I tried to avoid the question by changing the subject, he called me out on it. But I didn't want to antagonize him, you know. After all, he was a paying customer, and he was *the* Robert Ross. But I did ask the captain to assign me some other task and let someone else take over from having to serve him. But then he kept asking for me and accusing the captain of trying to hide me from him. So in the end there was no way around it, unless I resigned. And that wasn't going to happen because I need this job."

"He didn't actually... go any further, did he?" asked Odelia gently.

"What do you mean?" asked Suzanne with a frown.

"Well, did he try to kiss you? Or touch you?"

She thought for a moment, then nodded. "Once. But at that point, I'd become quite good at avoiding him, so I more or less ducked and made sure to get as far away from him as fast as I could. He complained, of course. Said I wasn't doing my job properly. And when Captain Gerard confronted him about the attempted kiss, he said it was just a joke, and I shouldn't make a mountain out of a molehill."

"But apart from that, nothing happened?"

She shook her head. "No, nothing. Though like I said, it was a drag having to work for the guy. Which is weird since I've always been a big fan, and so have my parents and my whole family and all of my friends. In fact, when they first heard I'd be working on the Aurora, they were almost as excited as I was that I was going to meet an actual star, you know. Only it didn't exactly turn out like that."

"Do you have any idea, Suzanne, who Mr. Ross was meeting this morning at ten o'clock?"

She shrugged. "No idea. He wanted us all off the boat, which was strange since he couldn't even open his own curtains in the morning or get out of bed. But now all of a sudden, he wanted the Aurora all to himself? We figured he was probably meeting some woman he had met in town and didn't want anyone to know about it, which probably meant one of two things. Either she was an escort or she was married. But either way, I don't know who it was." She leaned forward now, a look of interest having appeared in her eyes. "Why, do you think this mystery guest is the one who's involved in Robert dying somehow?"

"We're not sure," said Chase. "But what we do know is that this person might be the last person who saw Mr. Ross alive, and so we really need to speak to him or her." He gave the girl his card. "If you can think of anything else, Suzanne, or you hear something, please get in touch. It's important."

Her eyes had gone a little wide now. "Oh, my God. So it is true. Robert was murdered."

"Would that surprise you?" asked Odelia.

"Of course it would. I thought he drowned. But if he was murdered..." Her voice trailed off, and I wondered what she was thinking.

Chase must have wondered the same thing, for he asked, "Can you think of anyone who might have held a grudge against Mr. Ross, Suzanne?"

She quickly shook her head. Too quickly, I thought. "No idea. Can I go now?"

We watched her leave, and as Chase and Odelia shared a significant look, so did Dooley and I.

"I think she's the one, Max," said my friend.

"You think she murdered Robert Ross?"

"No, I think she stole our litter!"

CHAPTER 8

"What litter? What are you talking about?"

"The litter monster! It's her! I'm sure of it, Max."

I saw he was pointing to the floor of the mess, where all manner of litter had gathered over the course of the different interviews Chase and Odelia had conducted.

"It fell off her shoes," said Dooley. "I swear, Max. It wasn't there before, and now it's there, so it must have fallen off her shoes."

We both approached the litter, and I had to admit it did indeed look like the type of litter that we like to use in our litter boxes at home. It even smelled the same.

"But how?" I said. "And more importantly, why? Why would this Suzanne Palmer steal our litter?"

"I'm not sure," said Dooley. "But I intend to find out, Max."

"That's great, buddy," I said. "You find out who's been stealing our litter, and I'll try and find out who killed Robert Ross."

"Or..." he said, his tail quivering with excitement, "we could discover that it was one and the same person!"

"That seems highly unlikely, Dooley," I said. "Now why would Robert Ross's killer steal our litter?"

"Like I said, I don't know, but I'm going to find out. Just you wait and see!"

I gave him my most encouraging smile. "Keep me informed," was all I could find to say. A little lame, I know, but somehow apropos.

Before long, the interviews were at an end, and to be honest, we weren't a lot wiser than we had been before. Mr. Ross liked to keep himself to himself, except when it came to inviting pretty young servers to his suite and complaining when they turned him down. So we set paw for his suite in question to see if we could find some more clues as to the man's personality, his life and death, and most importantly, who had brought that about.

As expected, the actor's suite was the most luxurious one on the vessel and also the most spacious one. It offered a great view of the vessel's surroundings, located as it was on the middle deck, and effectively had windows all around. In actual fact, it wasn't one room but several, all comprising a single suite. Chase quickly started digging around for clues, even though the techies had already been there and had done the same thing. But then Odelia's husband is nothing if not meticulous and likes to be hands-on in every investigation he leads.

The actor's laptop had already been retrieved, as well as his phone, but our humans now checked his other personal belongings. They rifled through his clothes, checked the bathroom for any pillboxes containing medication that might prove interesting and shed light on the man's life, and generally went through the guy's personal stuff with a fine-tooth comb. Before long, Chase was holding up a book. It was a biography of Napoleon and had been thoroughly thumbed through, with even markers stuck to different pages indicating they held particular importance to the guy.

"I think he was probably preparing for a film role," said Odelia as she, in turn, held up a film script. It bore the title 'Napoleon and Josephine,' indicating that the actor, after playing James Fox for many years, was moving on to other parts.

"Several markings," she said as she leafed through the script. "Looks like he's been learning lines and preparing for the role." She studied the front page. "Director is Jack Foss. Producer Joshua Cunningham."

"Let's get their contact details and get in touch with them," Chase suggested. "If Ross was stepping out of the James Fox role, that might be important."

I saw that Dooley was intently sniffing about, clearly looking for something. "Looking for litter, buddy?" I asked.

"Well, I seem to have picked up the same smell, Max," he said. "But I can't be sure. Can you take a sniff and tell me what you think?"

"Sure," I said and sniffed where he told me to sniff. And I had to admit that he was right. There were indeed more traces of our litter on the floor near the bathroom. As if somehow Robert had stepped in litter and it had stuck to his feet or shoes and come off on the carpet. Though of course, it could have been a visitor.

"I think our litter thief has been here, Max," Dooley said now. "See? It's the same type of litter and the exact same smell."

"You're right, Dooley," I said. And so we approached Odelia with the view to tell her about Dooley's find, but unfortunately, she was in conversation with a member of the CSI team, discussing ways and means of processing both the

Napoleon book and movie script without the evidence being contaminated.

"I think our litter find is probably more important than this Napoleon business, Max," said Dooley.

"I'm not so sure. If Ross was taking on another part, that might have had an impact on his commitment to the James Fox role, and that might have made certain people very unhappy."

"Well, we have to tell Odelia about Suzanne," said Dooley. "Before she escapes, never to be seen again."

Chase and Odelia had told the crew not to leave town, but of course, that would be hard to enforce. Captain Gerard had asked if they could stay on the vessel until the investigation was concluded, but since it was a crime scene, that wasn't possible. Though Chase had promised they'd try to conclude their investigation as soon as possible. And so, most of the crew had decided to book into a hotel for the time being, where they could be reached if necessary.

We continued our own investigation and soon found more traces of litter, this time underneath the window. Apparently, whoever had carried the litter into the room had at some point stood by the window looking out, and also by the bathroom door. They had certainly used plenty of litter, and since as far as I could tell there were no cats on board, I wondered where that litter could have come from.

The answer soon became clear to us when we entered a sort of annex to the main room of the suite, and found... a litter box! And inside this litter box sat a small Papillon dog who answered to the name Flame.

We both turned our backs to her, allowing her to do her business in peace and comfort, then when we heard she had finished, we turned around again.

"So you have a litter box," said Dooley, and it sounded as if we had caught Flame in a very grave act of wrongdoing.

"Of course I have a litter box," said Flame. "You don't expect me to do my business on one of the decks, do you? Or, God forbid, in the pool?"

"No, I guess not," said Dooley as he gave this some thought. Clearly, he had never wondered how dogs travel on these yachts and where they do their business. And frankly, I had never wondered myself. But Flame was right. It's not as if there are lampposts aboard a vessel like the Aurora, or trees to do your business against.

"Okay, so we found traces of litter all over the living area," I said, deciding to take the interview in hand.

"And also in the mess," Dooley added, "right after Suzanne Palmer had walked there. So can you explain that, Flame?"

Flame smiled. "I don't have to explain anything. Suzanne was the person who cleaned out my litter box every day, so it stands to reason she would have some on her shoes. And as far as litter in the living room is concerned, I also have litter on my paws every time I leave my box, don't you?" She arched an inquisitive eyebrow, and I could have told her that cats don't share their trade secrets with dogs, but since the only way to get her to open up was to open up ourselves, I decided to confess.

"Yes, we do track litter all over the house, even though we try very hard to avoid it, but inevitably, the stuff will stick to our paws and get tracked all around."

"Same here," said Flame. "Litter gets stuck to my paws, and so it spreads all over the place."

"Oh," said Dooley, looking much disappointed that his theory about Suzanne being his litter monster looked like a dead end.

"So where is Harriet?" asked Flame, who apparently had become attached to our Persian friend.

"In town investigating the murder of your human," I said.

"We decided to split up so we can pursue multiple leads at the same time."

"Good thinking," she said. "Okay, so there is something I forgot to mention when I was talking to her."

"Oh?"

"Yeah, the thing is that even though Robert was very attached to his privacy and didn't have a lot of friends, he did have one good friend he'd known forever."

"Name?" I asked.

"Sebastian Poe. The odd thing is that I saw Sebastian last night when he paid us a visit."

"And why is that so odd?" I asked.

She shrugged. "Because Sebastian died a couple of weeks ago."

CHAPTER 9

Caroline Poots had been cleaning the kitchen counter with a dishrag when she happened to glance out of the kitchen window and saw an old lady and two cats pass by her house. She stared at the strange spectacle for a moment, wondering what they were up to. Mostly what she saw on any given day were dog owners walking their dogs, but she had never seen anyone walking their cats. And the cats were gorgeous: one was a white Persian, and the other a big, butch black one that looked like a real bruiser. The old lady looked vaguely familiar, as if she had seen her somewhere before, and then she had it. It was that ornery receptionist she sometimes saw when she went to the doctor. Rumor had it that she was Doctor Poole's mother-in-law, which had always struck her as a sad thing, since Doctor Poole was such a nice man—so warm and understanding—and then he was saddled with this annoying harridan for a mother-in-law. And not just that, but also his receptionist. Once she had even told the doctor that he should pick another receptionist because some people might be scared off by the one he had. But Doctor Poole had said the only way he could get a different

49

receptionist was if he murdered the one he had, and it hadn't even sounded as if he was joking!

"Poor man," she now said as she rinsed the dishrag and draped it over the rack.

"What did you say, sweetie?" asked her husband, who was drinking a cup of coffee and reading his paper.

"It's that receptionist of Doctor Poole," she said. "She just passed by on the street with two cats in tow. And I was just thinking that Doctor Poole should really do something about her, since she's just about the meanest old woman I've ever met in my life. Every time you call, she acts as if you've just disturbed her doing something a lot more important than taking your call. And then when you come in, she just looks at you as if you're something that's stuck to the bottom of her shoe and she'd much rather you hadn't come in at all."

"Yeah, she's just the worst, isn't she?" said Kirk, folding his paper. "Do you know that the last time I went in to see Doctor Poole, when I had that pain in my foot, and I told her about it, she said I should just chop it off if it was bothering me so much?" He laughed. "Chop off my foot!"

"People like that shouldn't be allowed to work in a doctor's office," said Caroline with a shake of the head. "There should be a law against it."

"Well, she does keep the hypochondriacs away. You have to be really, really sick to decide to brave that horrible woman to go and see the doctor."

But Caroline shook her head. "It's a nice theory, but it doesn't work like that, honey. Remember Ida Baumgartner? She's got all the diseases that have ever existed, and none of them are real. And still, she goes in and sees Doctor Poole all the time. Every time I go in, she's right there, explaining in excruciating detail about some new disease she just got. So no, if the doctor put his mother-in-law in place as some kind of gatekeeper, it's not working."

"Oh, well, at least we have a good doctor, even if he has lousy tastes in receptionists."

"It's not his fault. It's one of those curses a person has to bear."

And having said that, she put the phenomenon out of her head. Or at least she would have if not for the doorbell ringing, and she and her husband sharing a look of surprise.

"Now who can that be?" asked Kirk.

"Postman, probably," said Caroline.

But when she went to open the door, who did she find on the doorstep, looking at her as if she was a piece of poo stuck to the bottom of her shoe? None other than Vesta Muffin, accompanied by two cats, one black and one white.

"Caroline Poots?" asked the woman.

"That's right," said Caroline, much surprised by this visit. She stared at the cats, and it could just be her imagination, or they were staring back at her in much the same way Mrs. Muffin was.

"You're the head of the Chamber of Commerce committee that decides on the awards being given for the best Hampton Cove businesses?"

"Business of the year," she said. "Yes, I'm the chair of that committee." She wondered if Mrs. Muffin was going to ask to select her son-in-law for a prize. Caroline didn't know if the doctor was eligible, but having to put up with this woman, he might be eligible for the prize for a good Samaritan. Or maybe even a saint!

"Well, the thing is," said Mrs. Muffin, "that the winner of this year's award has just been murdered, and they've asked me to poke around and collect some impressions from people who knew the guy. Just to try and paint a picture of what he was like, you know, for police purposes?"

Caroline eyed the woman with a look of absolute bewilderment. "You... work for the police now, Mrs. Muffin?"

The woman looked surprised. "Oh, have we met before?"

"Yes, we have. I'm a patient of Doctor Poole's."

Mrs. Muffin's eyes narrowed, and Caroline could see the little cogs in her brain, hidden under those deceptively sweet-looking little white curls, working at full capacity. Then her face cleared. "Of course!" she said, pointing a finger at her. "Gallbladder!"

"Gallbladder?"

"I'm terrible at remembering names, so I just associate patients with their diseases, and for some reason, your face has gallbladder written all over it." Caroline's face must have betrayed her extreme dismay at being categorized in such a disrespectful way, so she amended, "Could be an ulcer, of course. Tex has so many patients, I get confused. But anyway, what can you tell me about Robert Ross? Have you met the guy? Did he hit on you?"

"Hit on me!"

"My granddaughter is conducting the actual investigation into the murder—or at least assisting the detective, who's her husband—and she tells me that Robert liked to hit on women. Hence the question."

Caroline blinked a few times. She was having a hard time coming to grips with the conversation as it was developing. This was the first she'd heard that Mr. Ross had died— murdered even—and here stood this annoying woman asking her all kinds of questions about the guy. "No, he has never 'hit' on me," she finally managed. "Look, do you work for the police or not?"

"Absolutely," said Mrs. Muffin proudly.

"Can you show some ID?" She found it extremely unlikely that the woman would suddenly go from being a receptionist to working as a police detective.

"No need!" said Vesta blithely. "My son is the chief of

police. So that gives me all the credentials I need to run any investigation I want."

"I... don't think it works like that, exactly. I'm pretty sure giving birth to a police officer doesn't make you a police officer yourself."

"Not a police officer. Alec is the *chief* of police."

"I know. But that doesn't make you the chief of police. Qualifications and experience don't travel up the hereditary line to a parent. If that were true, a president's mother would also be a president, a doctor's father a doctor and a Nobel-Prize-winning scientist's mom a scientist."

"Okay, so that's your opinion," said Vesta, "and of course, I respect your opinion, but that's not how I see it. And besides, it strikes me as significant that you're skirting the issue here." She fixed her with those beady eyes of hers. "What have you got to hide..." She glanced down at her phone. "Caroline Poots? Cause that's your name, isn't it? Caroline Poots?"

"That is my name," Caroline confirmed. "And I've got nothing to hide. But I do like to speak to an actual detective, and not my doctor's receptionist when I answer any questions. Because as far as I know, that's how things are done in a murder inquiry. Are you sure it was murder, by the way?"

"Absolutely," said Vesta. "I saw the dead guy myself. And I listened to, um, well someone who knows, explain exactly how he was murdered: poisoned. With cyanide, most likely." She took a step closer and sniffed. "Did you know that cyanide smells like almonds?"

"No, I did not know that," Caroline confessed.

"You smell like almonds, Caroline."

"That's probably because I just ate almonds."

"A likely story," Vesta scoffed. She now took a step back and shouted, "Caroline Poots, I'm arresting you on suspicion of the murder of Robert Ross!"

"What!"

"You have the right to... oh, heck, how did that go again? You watch a ton of crime shows and then when you need it, it's all gone. Anyway, you better come with me to the station so I can question you."

"I will do no such thing!"

"Then I'm afraid I'll have to use violence." She held up her arms in a pugilistic stance. "I'll have you know I've got a black belt in karate."

"Be that as it may, but I'm not going anywhere with you. You're not a cop, you can't go around arresting people. You can't even interrogate people like this!"

"I think you'll find that I can... Miss Gallbladder!"

Behind her, Kirk had appeared. He looked mildly amused, which told Caroline that he must have followed the interaction. "Mrs. Muffin," he said. "What seems to be the problem?"

"*You're* the gallbladder!" said Vesta, pointing an accusing finger at Caroline's husband.

"I think you'll find I'm the migraine sufferer."

"Oh," said Vesta. "Well, my bad. So how are you involved in all of this..."

"Kirk," he said helpfully. "Kirk Poots. Well, I'm married to Caroline, who works for the Chamber of Commerce, and in that capacity decided to award a prize to Robert Ross. But apart from that, we never actually met the man. Not me and not Caroline. All this was handled by Mr. Ross's manager."

"Agent," Caroline corrected him.

"Big Hollywood stars like Mr. Ross don't deal with these matters personally," Kirk explained. "As a representative of the Hampton Cove Chamber of Commerce, you decide to award a prize, so you contact the man's agent or manager, and everything is arranged by them. And then, if you're lucky, the star in question will show up on the day and collect his award. Though more often than not, he will not show up and will send the agent or manager."

"So you never met Ross?" asked Vesta, sounding and looking disappointed.

Both Caroline and her husband shook their heads.

"Never met the man in my life," Caroline confirmed.

"So he never hit on you?"

"He never hit on me."

"Oh."

For a moment, no one spoke, then Kirk cleared his throat. "So is my wife still under arrest?"

But Vesta's mind seemed to have leaped to other pastures, like a nimble mountain goat jumping from crag to crag. She made a throwaway gesture with her hand. "Nah, that's all off," she said vaguely. "So can you think of anyone who might bear a grudge against the guy?"

"Not really," said Caroline. "Because I don't know him."

"Never met him," Kirk repeated in kindly tones.

"So... why did you decide to give him this award?"

Caroline took a deep breath. "Because he was born in Hampton Cove, even though he left to pursue an acting career at an early age."

"I think he was eighteen when he left home," said Kirk.

"But the fact remains that he's a Hampton Covian, and with the success he's had, we've been wanting him to accept this award for a long time. Only he never seemed interested."

"So you contacted him before?"

"Oh, absolutely. The first time we got in touch with Mr. Ross's team was fifteen years ago when he first landed the James Fox role and became a star and a household name. But he refused. We've asked him every year since, and every time he said he wasn't interested."

"Until this year."

"Until this year," Caroline confirmed, though she wondered why she was even talking to this ridiculous woman. Sooner or later, a real police detective would probably show up and ask them the same questions. Then again, maybe not. If he allowed this woman to run loose and harass people, clearly Chief Lip wasn't running the tight ship Caroline had always supposed he did.

"So what made him change his mind?"

"No idea."

"We've been asking ourselves the same question," Kirk intimated.

"It's puzzling," said Vesta as she took out a notebook from her pocket and scribbled down a couple of notes. She then gave them a cheerful smile. "Well, that's all, folks. If I think of something else, I'll be back. Until then, cheerio!"

"Cheerio," said Kirk, earning himself a scowl from his wife.

When they closed the door, she thought she heard Vesta's cats say something in their cat language. And oddly enough, Vesta actually talked back to them!

"The woman is certifiable," she told Kirk.

"She's quite a colorful character, isn't she?"

"Colorful isn't the word I would use."

"So Robert is dead?"

"Murdered."

"How about that?"

They shared a look. "I wonder if Jane knows."

CHAPTER 10

"I think you made an indelible impression on that woman, Gran," said Harriet.

"Yeah, she really spilled the beans, didn't she?" asked Brutus.

"Oh, well," said Vesta modestly. "Sometimes you have to be tough with these people. It's the only way to get them to talk." She, too, was pleased with the way her first interview had gone. When Odelia had asked her to talk to people who may have known Robert Ross, she had experienced one of those very rare—for her, at least—attacks of self-doubt, wondering if she'd be able to crack these people and make them talk turkey. But that business about arresting Miss Gallbladder had done the trick. Good cop, bad cop all rolled into one!

"So Mr. Ross never wanted that award, and then suddenly this year he did?" asked Harriet. "Doesn't that strike you as significant, Gran?"

"It most certainly does, Harriet. I think we just got our very first clue. And if I'm not mistaken, this just might blow this whole case wide open!"

"Well done, Gran," said Brutus with genuine admiration in his voice.

"It's all those years working as a receptionist," she said. "You learn to read people, you know, read them like a book. Now take this Poots woman, for instance. I knew the moment I laid eyes on her that she was going to be a tough nut to crack, so I had to go in guns blazing, put the fear of God into her. And good thing I did, for she started singing like a canary as soon as the prospect of spending the night in a cold, uncomfortable police cell was raised."

"Were you really going to arrest her, Gran?" asked Harriet.

"Of course I was! Idle threats fool no one, and she would have seen right through me. I had to make it real, or it wouldn't have worked." She took out her phone and moments later was in contact with Odelia. "Honey, I just blew this whole case wide open." And as she proceeded to explain to her granddaughter how her first interview had gone, she was satisfied to note that Odelia was as intrigued as she was by Robert's sudden about-face where that award was concerned. "I'll keep talking to people," she promised. "And I'll keep chipping away at this case bit by bit, piece by piece, until I've got my hands on that killer!"

"Please be careful, Gran," said Odelia. "If Robert's murderer realizes that you're on to him, he might strike out, like a caged animal."

"Don't you worry about that, honey," she said. "I've got Harriet and Brutus with me, and they'll protect me from this maniac, I'm sure."

Though when she glanced down at her cats, they didn't seem as sanguine as she was about their capacity for stopping a murderer. Luckily she had faith enough for three. She hung up after once again promising her granddaughter that she would be careful. She had arrived at her next witness.

This time it was one of the people supplying food to the ship's cook on a regular basis. It didn't seem like a high-profile witness, not the way Caroline Poots had been, but still, it was important to talk to everybody, from the lowliest to the most important, and since she had a job to do, she pressed her finger to the buzzer and got on with it.

* * *

ODELIA GAVE her husband a look of concern. They had just finished talking to the chef who had prepared meals for the star but also for the crew, but unfortunately, the man hadn't given them anything they didn't already know.

"What?" asked Chase, catching her look.

"Remember I asked my grandmother to go and talk to people who might have seen Robert?"

"To get her off the boat and stop messing with our investigation? Sure."

"Well, now she's actually interviewing people and representing herself as a member of the police force, which of course she is not."

Chase's expression clouded. "She shouldn't do that. It's going to mess even more with our investigation than if she had simply remained on board and stuck her nose where it didn't belong."

"I know, but I thought it couldn't do any harm if she simply talked to a couple of people in town, you know, like shopkeepers that maybe served Robert at some point over the course of the last week. Pick up gossip about what people thought of him and such. But instead, she's actually talking to potential witnesses and inserting herself into the investigation big-time."

Chase actually grinned at this. "She reminds me of a

certain person who also used to insert herself into my investigations all the time."

"Oh?" she said innocently. "I have no idea who you're talking about."

"A certain someone who, in spite of the fact that I told her off in no uncertain terms on many occasions, still persisted. And as a consequence, ended up solving more than a few murders."

"Well, Gran isn't me, Chase. She has a way to go about things that puts people's backs up."

"You put my back up when I first arrived in Hampton Cove," he reminded her.

"That was different. You came from a different background, where you didn't think members of the general public could be helpful in your investigations."

"And yet you proved time and again that you were. So helpful that I've often wondered if we shouldn't send you to the police academy to make an honest cop out of you."

"I'm a reporter first and foremost, Chase," she reminded him. "If I wanted to be a cop, I would have said yes to my uncle's suggestion years ago."

He arched an eyebrow. "Alec suggested you become a cop?"

"Of course. Many times. But I love being a reporter. In fact, I love the way things are now: as a police consultant, I get to participate—"

"Meddle."

"*Participate* in any investigation where I'm needed—"

"And even those where you're not."

She gave him a grin. "You love it."

"I do," he admitted. "I think you have a knack. Though without the assistance of your cats, I'm not sure your success rate would be quite as high as it is now."

They glanced down to where Max and Dooley were

intently listening to their conversation. They were still in the mess, and as far as Odelia could tell, had spoken to all the crew members, with her cats listening in and providing an occasional comment. Unfortunately, nobody had presented them with a clue that would 'break this case wide open,' as Gran had termed it.

Chase's officers had also searched all the cabins—in fact, they had searched the entire vessel—but so far hadn't found anything of note. No little vial with cyanide hidden underneath someone's mattress. No threatening letters. No diary revealing a long history of harassment on Mr. Ross's part, causing the killer to see no alternative but to get rid of the man once and for all.

"So what do you think, Max?" she asked now. "Any leads?"

"Nothing," said Max disappointingly. "As far as I can tell, Robert Ross was not very well-liked by his crew members. He acted cold and aloof and treated them like serfs and underlings, demanding they didn't look him in the eye and pretend to be invisible, except when he needed them to wait on him hand and foot as if he was some kind of lord and master. And he kept harassing Suzanne Palmer to the point she might have to quit her job. Not a nice man."

"No, I think we can all agree that he was a real piece of work."

"And the litter mystery has also been solved," Dooley pointed out. "It was Suzanne who tracked that litter all over the cabin and also the ship when she changed Flame's litter box."

She turned to her husband. "We should look into this Sebastian Poe business, babe. A dead man who shows up the day before his best friend is murdered? I wonder what that was all about."

"Already on it," said Chase as he texted a message on his phone, presumably instructing one of his officers to dig a little deeper into Sebastian Poe's relationship with Robert Ross. When Max had brought the man to their attention, they had asked the crew members about it, but none of them had clapped eyes on this childhood friend. So Odelia was inclined to think that either Flame was mistaken or that Robert had invited Poe on board during one of those moments he'd demanded to be left alone, which had happened more and more often. As if there were people he wanted to meet that he didn't want the members of the ship's crew to know about.

A man like Robert Ross was, of course, very attached to his privacy, and all the crew members had signed a non-disclosure agreement before they were hired. But even so, it was probably hard to determine who had leaked certain information to the media. Or even tipped off a paparazzo to snap a couple of pictures of this or that person boarding the vessel to meet with Robert. After having been a major international movie star, the man had become a little para-noid, and possibly with good reason.

"Okay, so where are we?" asked Chase, stretching for a moment, his back crackling as he did.

"We know that Robert probably died around ten o'clock, possibly from cyanide poisoning, after sending the crew off the ship, possibly because he was meeting someone, though we can't be sure that he was."

"A lot of possibly's and probably's," Chase grunted.

It was true that, even though they had talked to all the crew members, they still didn't have a lot of information about what happened that morning. Even Robert's dog, Flame, apparently hadn't seen this mystery guest Robert was supposedly meeting since she was being walked at the time. So not only had Robert sent all the crew members ashore, but even his own dog. How odd was that? Or maybe it was simply a coincidence.

CHAPTER 11

$\mathcal{W}$e left the Aurora feeling a little puzzled. Odelia and Chase were puzzled by the mystery of the death of the famous actor. Dooley was puzzled by the mystery of the litter monster, whose identity he thought he had finally solved but had to admit had eluded him once more. And I was puzzled by the fact that I hadn't had a nap in hours and still felt more or less functional. Then again, they always say you probably need a lot less sleep than you think you do, so maybe that was the answer to that particular riddle.

Chase decided to head to the police station to work on his report of the different interviews they had conducted. Odelia set foot for the *Gazette* offices to work on an article about the murder, always keeping in mind that she should not disclose information crucial to the investigation. And Dooley and I? Well, we were in a quandary for a moment.

My first inclination was to follow Odelia and take a long and much-deserved nap in her office, as we often do, and allow inspiration to come to us, which it invariably does. Then again, I had this feeling we probably wouldn't be getting any sleep at all, for Odelia would be on the phone talking to people and interrupting our pleasant slumber. So instead, we decided to head home where we could nap in absolute peace and quiet. And since the road home led past the General Store, we popped in to say hi to Kingman and ask if he'd heard anything worth reporting about this murder business.

Kingman was chatting with Buster, the tabby belonging to Fido Siniawski, the hair stylist who coifs pretty much everyone in town, including but not limited to all of our own family members.

"I just heard," said Buster in a sort of breathless way. "James Fox! Murdered! How is that even possible! I thought James Fox couldn't die!"

"James Fox did die," said Kingman, and when Buster gazed at him in horror, he shrugged. "I'm sorry if this is a spoiler, but in his last movie James Fox did actually die. Though I'm sure he'll still be back. Not sure how, but then Hollywood is great at reviving people, so they'll probably find a way."

"Well, Robert Ross also died," I said, "and that's because he's a human person, or was, and James Fox is not. He's just a character created by a writer."

"Well, I know that, of course," said Buster with a laugh. "But still..." He was quiet for a moment, as we all were. It isn't every day that James Fox, or at least the actor playing James Fox, dies. And not even in a firefight with the evil Dr. Maybe or because he sets off some huge bomb or something, but simply because he is poisoned, then thrown into his own pool.

"So did you hear anything about this?" I asked Kingman.

"Well..." The big cat hesitated.

"Yes?" I asked encouragingly.

"Rumor has it that Robert had a sweetheart in town, though nobody knows who she is."

"A sweetheart? You mean like a girlfriend?"

"Like sailors have girlfriends in every port," said Kingman, "Ross had a girlfriend in every country. And in this country, his girlfriend happened to live in Hampton Cove, though, to be honest, I very much doubt that to be the case. But for what it's worth, I still registered the information, knowing sooner or later you'd show up and ask me all about it." He took a deep breath and launched into his tale. "Okay, so from what I've heard, Robert Ross, long before he became *the* Robert Ross, was dating his high school sweetheart. Only something happened, and they broke up. At which point Robert decided to take his broken heart and leave town. Only to come back many years later as a rich and famous movie star."

"So who's the girl?" I asked.

But Kingman shook his head. "I didn't get any names. Only that they went to school together, and they were high school sweethearts, and everyone thought they were going to get married, but then they didn't."

"Maybe that's the reason Robert finally decided to pick up his award," I told Dooley. For Kingman and Buster's sake, I reiterated what Gran had told Odelia over the phone about the Chamber of Commerce thing. That Ross had refused the award for fifteen years in a row before finally accepting it this year.

"Maybe he figured he wasn't famous enough yet," Kingman ventured. "Figured he needed to be really famous before returning to the town where his heart was broken."

"Or maybe he simply didn't want to face his high school sweetheart," said Buster. "And finally, his manager told him that he couldn't keep putting it off, so he said yes."

"Do you think they ended up meeting again?" asked

65

Dooley. Then his eyes went wide. "Max! Maybe she was the mystery guest! The one he told his crew to go ashore for so he could meet her in private. And then she killed him!"

"It's possible," I allowed. It was imperative we got a name, though. Which probably wouldn't be all that hard for Chase and Odelia, since Ross and the girl had been in school together, so other kids in their year must have known all about this ill-fated romance.

"I think it's all very romantic," said Buster fervently. "Local boy done good returns to his long-lost love. Maybe they fell in love all over again before some mysterious hand struck him down."

"I'm with Dooley on this one," said Kingman. "I'll bet it was her hand that struck him down. Probably because he knew too much about her."

"What could he possibly know about her that caused her to murder him fifteen or more years after the fact?" I asked.

"How old was Ross?" asked Kingman.

"Um... forty-three," I said.

"If he left town at eighteen, that means they broke up twenty-five years ago, Max, not fifteen."

"So you're looking for Robert Ross's forty-three-year-old ex-girlfriend," said Buster. "Shouldn't be hard, especially for your policeman human, Max."

"No, I can't imagine Chase would find it hard to determine the identity of this woman," I agreed.

"I just hope she has cats or a dog," said Dooley. "Though preferably cats, of course, since cats never lie, and dogs do. They're treacherous that way."

"Dogs lie? What makes you say that?" asked Buster.

"Well, we talked to Robert's dog," Dooley explained. "And she claimed to know nothing about either the murder or the visit of this person this morning. Which is very unlikely, as dogs always know." He gave us a knowing look. "They have an instinct about their humans, so they know. But they're also fiercely loyal, so they will never talk. And so they will lie when asked to spill the beans, just like Flame did."

"Flame, is that the dog's name?" Kingman wanted to know.

Dooley nodded. "And I still think she was lying about that litter. I'm pretty sure she knows all about the litter monster, but she simply chose to protect her for some reason that I haven't figured out yet. But I'm going to," he promised.

Oh, dear.

CHAPTER 12

*H*arriet had been prancing along next to her boyfriend Brutus and Gran when, all of a sudden, she had an idea. One of those bright ideas she got all the time. Though it probably wasn't too much to say it was a brilliant one. And so she told Brutus, "I think I know who killed Robert Ross, honey bunny."

"Yeah, who?" asked Brutus in that customary slightly gruff way of his that she liked so much. He was, after all, a real cat's cat—a hero of many battles. One could even say that he was the Humphrey Bogart of cats and wouldn't have been out of place in one of that man's movies, donning the actor's trademark hat and looking very butch. Okay, so maybe not.

"Suzanne Palmer!" said Harriet. "So we know that the guy had been harassing her non-stop from the moment she joined the crew, right?"

"Right."

"So what if he actually took things one step further one night and actually assaulted her? And then Suzanne, instead of going to the cops, since she knew that Robert was a powerful and famous man and they might not believe her, talked to the captain instead. And the captain told the rest of the crew, and they all banded together to conspire to kill their colleague's tormentor."

She gave her partner a triumphant look, fully expecting him to applaud her brilliant deduction. But instead, he grimaced. "Doubtful," he told her.

"What!"

"Honey muffin, in this day and age, movie actors aren't as powerful as they used to be, and they sure as heck can't get away with something like that, especially when the rest of the crew is prepared to testify on Suzanne's behalf. So as attractive as your theory sounds, I don't think that's what happened."

"Well, I do," she said stubbornly. "In fact, I'm prepared to bet on it."

He grinned. "What do you want to bet?"

"I'll bet that it's actually one of our humans who has done away with our litter."

"You think so? But why?"

"To save money, of course. Do you know how expensive cat litter is? They probably didn't want to admit that they've decided to economize, so they simply emptied our litter boxes, forcing us to do our business out in Blake's Field."

"But if that's true, that means that we'll have to continue using Blake's Field from now on. Always!"

She nodded slowly. It was a terrifying prospect since she, especially, had to tinkle all the time. And if she had to traipse all the way over to Blake's Field every time she had to answer nature's call, it was going to seriously cut into her nap time.

"So maybe we should look for an alternative," she now said.

"Like what?"

"Well, if they're so determined to make us do our business

outside, why don't we use their precious rose bushes from now on? I'll bet that if we consistently do this, the four of us, our litter will make a sudden and unexplained comeback, and we won't have to go to Blake's Field anymore."

He eyed her with admiration written all over his features. Now this was the kind of look she liked to see on her boyfriend's face. The look that said she was the smartest cat on the block. Okay, so maybe not the smartest, for that was Max, paws down, but at least the most resourceful one. She was willing to bet that even Max couldn't have hit on such a brilliant solution to a problem that had been vexing them since that morning when they first discovered their litter boxes devoid of one of its most important ingredients, not to mention its raison d'être, namely litter.

"That's the most brilliant thing I've ever heard, honey plum," he said. "I'll bet it won't take more than a day, two tops, before our litter is back where it belongs: in our boxes, ready to process, with a capacity of forty times its own weight, the products of our bladder and bowel movements."

They had arrived at the Star Hotel, where Gran had decided to take a load off her feet and meet up with her friend Scarlett. And as the two ladies took a seat at one of the tables in the outside dining area, Harriet and Brutus hoped they wouldn't forget about them and at the very least offer them a dish of water.

"So what's all this I hear about Robert Ross being murdered?" asked Scarlett as she sipped from her cappuccino.

"It's true," Gran confirmed. "Odelia found him floating in his pool this morning."

"The pool on his own private yacht," said Scarlett appreciatively.

"And a nice yacht it was," Gran confirmed. "One of those big fancy ones."

"So who did it?" asked Scarlett.

"That, we don't know yet," Gran confessed. "Though it wouldn't surprise me if the crew decided to band together and off the guy."

"The crew? But why? Was he such a horrible boss?"

"He was," Gran said. "Harassing poor innocent girls and generally being pretty uncool to the rest of the crew. So they poisoned him."

Harriet turned to her boyfriend. "See? I told you I was onto something."

"Mere speculation and hearsay," he said, sounding more like Perry Mason all of a sudden and less like Humphrey Bogart.

"I still think that's what happened, and obviously Gran thinks the same thing. We'll tell Max," she finally decided. "He'll know it's true."

"Mh," said Brutus noncommittally.

"What? You don't think Max will know?"

"Max always knows," said Brutus with a sigh, as if it was the bane of his existence.

There had been a time when Brutus decided to compete with Max as a detective, but he had soon admitted that no one could best their large blorange friend in that department. According to Dooley, it had something to do with the size of Max's head, which just might be true. A head that size must have been designed to accommodate a very large brain. And since Max often ate fish, and fish is known for its brain-enhancing qualities, that was Max's big secret revealed. Though it had to be said he really was very smart when it came to solving mysteries.

"Okay, so what have you discovered so far?" asked Scarlett.

"Only that for fifteen long years, Ross refused to return to Hampton Cove to pick up his prize from the Chamber of

Commerce until finally this year he decided to show up in person. But when I asked the committee chairwoman, who goes over this stuff, she had no idea what had changed his mind."

"Probably a woman," Scarlett suggested. "Only a woman has the power to make a man change his mind like that. He probably had a girl here he didn't want to see, and now he did."

"You mean, she died and so now he figured the coast was clear?"

"Something like that. He must have knocked her up back in the day, and so her dad and brothers chased him out of town with pitchforks. Only the dad died, and the brothers left, and so now he finally felt safe enough to return."

"That sounds a little far-fetched to me," said Gran. "Though it's possible, of course. Oh, and have you heard of a man named Sebastian Poe? Apparently, he was a childhood friend of Robert's who died. Only Robert's dog, Flame, saw him last night on the Aurora."

"A dead man paying a visit to a man who is soon found dead himself?"

"That's right. It all feels a little off, don't you agree? As if we're being led by the hand to some kind of foregone conclusion."

"See!" said Harriet. "I knew that dog Flame was feeding us a lot of nonsense. I'll bet she's been lying to us from the very beginning!"

Gran's phone chimed, and when she picked up, it soon became clear she was talking to her granddaughter. The words, 'Hey, Odelia, I was just telling Scarlett all about the investigation,' were probably a good indication of that.

She listened for a moment, then said in a low voice, "No way! That's exactly what Scarlett thought! Okay, we'll find this woman for you, honey, no problem." When she hung up, her eyes were glistening. "You were right, Scarlett. Robert did have a girlfriend, only he didn't knock her up, or at least that's not what Max heard, who told Odelia." And she proceeded to tell them all about what Max had heard from Kingman, who had heard it from one of his human's customers at the General Store, so it must be true!

"Oh, my God," said Scarlett, clutching her face in excitement. "It's almost like an episode of *General Hospital*!"

"I want you to join the investigation, honey," said Gran.

"What, me?"

"Absolutely. We're going to find this mystery woman for Odelia."

"Oh, goodie!"

"After all, the Hampton Cove Neighborhood Watch Committee can't just stand idly by while its citizens are being murdered in their beds, right?"

"Robert wasn't a citizen."

"He used to be."

"And he wasn't murdered in his bed."

"He could have been!"

And since that was good enough for Gran and Scarlett, it certainly was good enough for Harriet and Brutus. And so their select company of three had expanded to four. That's when Harriet decided to tell Gran all about her own brilliant theory about the killer. Gran didn't seem overly impressed but was willing to put Suzanne Palmer on her list of suspects, to be interviewed and interrogated at some point during her investigation.

Maybe they'd even crack this case before Max did this time.

Now, wouldn't that be something?

CHAPTER 13

*S*uzanne Palmer was glad the endless series of interviews was finally over. She had never been involved in a police investigation before, but now that she had, she decided she never wanted to go through that whole ordeal again. And now they couldn't even stay on the boat and have access to their personal belongings, just because the Aurora was apparently a crime scene. She didn't see how her own cabin was a crime scene since no crime had ever been committed there, except maybe some very bad thoughts she'd harbored about her employer, but also about some of her colleagues. Marcus O'Reilly, for one, had never been one of her favorites.

Shifty-eyed and with a mind full of malice, he always had some glib comment to make and generally struck her as a particularly obnoxious human being. But then you didn't choose the people you worked with and simply tried to make the best of the situation that you could. At least their captain had been a good guy. Jean-Luc Gerard was such a sweetheart it was a miracle he'd ever been made captain. Though of course, it wasn't as if he actually steered big cruise ships or anything. In all probability, he had simply taken a couple of courses and that was that. But he certainly was a sweetheart and had always been there for her when she needed a shoulder to cry on. And that had happened often enough, unfortunately.

But now their ordeal was finally over—or at least almost. Once the investigation had pinpointed who had murdered that horrible piece of excrement, they could all move on with their lives and hopefully put this whole sordid episode behind them.

She, for sure, was never going to think back to the weeks she had spent waiting on that monster. Then again, maybe she would. Gerard had told her that maybe she needed to consult a shrink so she could process what had happened. By all rights, she should sue the company that had put her on the same boat with that maniac. But then she knew she didn't stand a chance of winning. After all, she was just a lowly server, and Ross a big millionaire star. It would always have been her word against his, and no doubt the person who had the money to pay for the fancy lawyers invariably won. That's the way the game was rigged in their favor. At least that's what her colleague Jeanine had told her. Jeanine was an older colleague, probably in her late forties, which had surprised Suzanne when they first met since most of the colleagues she had worked with on other boats had been her age. Working on yachts for the super-rich was mostly a young person's game. When you got older, you tried to get a more solid gig with better pay and better hours—and clients who didn't treat you like dirt.

She smiled as Jeanine now joined her. They had arranged to meet for a cup of coffee in one of the new eateries in the New Marina, as the shopping plaza was called. They shared a quick hug before Jeanine sat down across from her.

"So how did it go?" she asked. "They didn't give you a hard time, did they?"

"Nope. They asked me a ton of questions, to which I invariably answered that I had no idea since it's my policy to keep a safe distance from any client I'm supposed to be working for. And that was it."

"And they accepted it?"

"What else could they do? If we all tell them the same story, they're bound to accept it, aren't they?"

It was true enough. Once they had become aware that Ross was dead, they had quickly shared the story in their WhatsApp group and had agreed, mainly on Gerard's instigation, to close ranks and not to divulge anything that might put them at odds with the police investigation that no doubt would follow and consume their lives for the foreseeable future. At that time, they hadn't known whether he'd been murdered or had simply died from natural causes, but the consensus had been that he was murdered, and good riddance too.

"I just hope they won't go digging any deeper," said Suzanne.

"Oh, they won't. They'll soon find their killer, and then this will all be over with."

"How can you be so sure?" asked Suzanne.

Jeanine gave her a fine smile. "Trust me, I know."

"You didn't do anything... I mean, you won't get into trouble, will you?"

"Of course not. It's got nothing to do with me, any of this. But I'm pretty sure they'll finally come to the conclusion that someone saw their chance to climb aboard, murdered the guy, and stole the sizable pile of cash he had lying around in that safe of his."

"And to think the fool thought we didn't know," said Suzanne.

"So what are you going to do once the investigation is over?" asked Jeanine.

She shrugged. "I was thinking of moving back home."

"North Dakota, right?"

"Yeah, that's right. Northwood." It might be the middle of nowhere, but frankly, that's what she was looking for more than anything right now. She'd had her adventure, had traveled with the rich and famous on their superyachts for three years now, and she was done. Done with the traveling, but most of all, done with the annoying clients and their never-ending demands and their shocking arrogance. She longed to be treated like a human being again, not a mere serf, eager to please and always ready to serve. When she had left home, she had been looking forward to traveling the world, making friends, and earning lots of money. Now all she wanted was to lick her wounds and think about her future in more practical terms. Which, at least, was something good that had come from the ordeal. "And you?"

"Oh, I don't know. I guess I'll keep going and hope to get some nice clients for a change. There are nice rich people out there somewhere, you know. Only we haven't met them yet."

"I hope you're right," she said with a smile. "We'll stay in touch, yeah?"

"Absolutely," said Jeanine and placed her hand on hers for a moment. They exchanged a look of understanding. Together they'd been through a lot and had come out the other end, alive and more or less fine. But as they had agreed with the others, they would never tell. Not to the police, not to anyone. What had happened on the Aurora would be their secret, always.

77

CHAPTER 14

*W*e had finally made it home, and I was about to enjoy my long-overdue and, as far as I was concerned, well-deserved nap when we were waylaid in the backyard by a loud voice demanding our attention. The voice belonged to Joe the caterpillar, and apparently he had a matter of some urgency to discuss with us.

So we joined him near the rose bushes posthaste and were quite surprised to see that where before one Joe had been, now about a dozen Joes perched. Or at least that's how it seemed to me at first glance.

"Are these... your twins?" I asked.

"Huh? Oh, they're my cousins," said Joe. "What I wanted to see you about, Max. Have you had a chance to chat with that Pesto scarecrow yet?"

"I talked to Gran, whose name is Vesta, by the way, and not Pesto, and I have agreed with her to try and dissuade you from using her rose bushes as food," I said. "So, without further ado: please don't use our humans' rose bushes as food. They don't like it, the roses don't like it— they might not even survive if you eat all of their leaves and nibble at their roots—and as a consequence, we also don't like it."

"But then what are we going to eat?" said Joe, much disappointed in my work as his emissary. "You don't expect us to eat grass, do you? Do you know how horrible that tastes?"

"I'm not a grass gourmet, that's true," I said. "Though I have been known to nibble on a blade from time to time. It turns my stomach, you see, and provides certain enzymes that are very beneficial to the overall digestive—"

"Well, I don't like grass!" said Joe. "And frankly speaking, Max, you can't force us to eat grass. Not only does it taste horrible, but it's not as nutritious as you would think. Not something your growing caterpillar needs."

"Is it true that you guys all turn into butterflies?" asked Dooley, who had been studying Joe and his cousins with rapt attention and not a small measure of delight.

"Butterflies or moths," Joe confirmed. "Though in our case, butterflies. Of course."

"Why of course?"

"Who wants to turn into a moth? I don't."

"But why?"

"Let me put it to you this way: do you want to be a moth?"

"Um... I guess I've never given it a lot of thought."

"Moths are not your most beloved creatures..."

"Dooley," Dooley supplied helpfully.

"They've got a bad reputation."

"I guess so."

"Whereas butterflies have a great reputation. Everybody likes butterflies. People love our colors, they love our shapes, and most of all, they love our devil-may-care attitude, fluttering from flower to flower with not a care in the world. In other words, butterflies are the 'it' bugs."

"And moths aren't?"

"If butterflies are it, moths are out, Dooley. People

associate moths with darkness and destruction. So no, I wouldn't want to be a moth. Not if you gave me a million bucks. Now back to the topic at hand. Max, you gotta convince that scarecrow—"

"Gran."

"Whatever—to leave us be. Tell her we'll be out of her hair soon enough when we all turn into butterflies, and she'll be glad she didn't zap us to kingdom come. She'll be delighted with the atmosphere of summery delight we bring to her backyard, and the fact that we pollinate stuff and generally are a boon for the environment. Plus, we look pretty cool."

"You do look cool," I admitted.

"So be patient, is what I would suggest to the scarecrow. Curb that tendency to spray us with that noxious stuff, and you'll be rewarded with a most gorgeous scene in just a few short weeks."

"How long before you turn into butterflies?" asked Dooley, the Discovery Channel fan.

"I'd say about a month or so for me. Some of these fellas might take a little longer. But all in all, by the time summer is here, we'll also be here. With bells on."

It certainly was a passionate plea, and I promised to be Joe's emissary when relaying his message to Gran. Though I was starting to feel like a go-between now, not all that sure I was doing a good job of conveying the messages I was receiving from either side of the great divide.

We said goodbye to Joe and his cousins and were about to enter the house when Grace came toddling up. "Hey, you guys," she said in that charming way of hers. "What's going on? Where are my mom and dad? And why haven't they dropped me off at the daycare as usual?"

"Because your daycare is closed today," I told the kid. "And it might be closed for the next couple of days as well, and even the foreseeable—and possibly the unforeseeable—future."

"But why?"

"No idea. Family circumstances, apparently. Whatever that means."

"Maybe Chantal is ill?" Dooley suggested. "Even daycare people get sick sometimes, Grace. And when they do, they can't take care of you."

Grace thought about this for a moment, then said, "I want to visit her."

We both looked up in alarm. "What?"

"I said I want to visit her. If she's sick, I should go and wish her well and maybe bring her flowers." She thought some more. "Or a banana."

"Grapes," said Dooley. "When people are sick, they always get grapes. Don't ask me why, but they do. My theory is that grapes have magical healing powers, but please don't quote me on that. It's only a theory. It would have to be tested before it becomes scientific fact."

"We could go and buy grapes now," Grace suggested, "and pay a visit to Chantal. She lives in the same house the daycare is at, so I know the way."

"You know the way to the daycare?"

"Of course. I pay attention, you know, when they take me there. So we could go now," she continued, giving me much the same kind of look Joe the caterpillar had given me earlier.

"We can't," I told her. "You're too young to venture out on your own."

"No, I'm not. And besides, I wouldn't be alone. You'd both be going with me."

"And Tex," Dooley pointed out. "Don't forget about Tex."

"Tex won't come," I said. "Because we won't be able to communicate to him that we want to visit the daycare."

"We could type it on our tablet," Dooley said. "That way he'll understand."

It was a thought, of course. I wasn't sure if it was doable, but it certainly merited a try since I could already see that there would be no naps in my immediate future.

"Oh, all right," I said with a sigh.

"Yay!" said Grace. "I knew you'd say yes!"

"That's because we always say yes," said Dooley happily, the pushover.

We went into the house to look for our tablet, which we found tucked behind the couch, where presumably Harriet had left it after her last session. When we started it up, the first thing I saw was a YouTube video about how to fashion the perfect bow for cats. I quickly switched to one of the note apps, and before long, we were typing a message to Tex. Grace then took the tablet and proceeded to carry it over into the garden next door to show to Tex, who was gazing intelligently into the middle distance, no doubt thinking about life and such.

When he became aware of Grace's presence because she had hit him in the shin with the tablet, after cursing a little, he took the tablet and made to deposit it on the table while the three of us tried to make it clear to him he should start it up and read what we had written.

It took us a while before he got the picture, but finally, he did start up the tablet and read, "Grace wants to pay a visit to Chantal. Please take us." He frowned at this, then his face morphed into an expression of delight. "Grace, you can write! What a genius!"

"What an idiot," Grace said as she thunked her head.

It didn't matter who had written the message, though, as long as it was clear, and that, it most certainly was. And since Tex has always been the amenable type, five minutes later we were all filing into his car and we took off in the direction of the daycare.

"I wonder how sick she is," said Grace with a note of concern in her voice. "I mean, if she's really sick, we should probably bring her more than just grapes, right?"

"Oh, the grapes!" said Dooley. "We should tell Tex about the grapes!"

And so we returned to the tablet and typed out another message. It took a while since we're not all that dexterous on a tablet, but we finally managed. Then Grace took the tablet and showed it to her grandfather. Tex, momentarily taking his eyes off the road, glanced down. "Grapes? Do you really think we should get her grapes?"

"You're a doctor, granddad," said Grace. "Maybe you can bring her some medicine that will make her feel better?"

But since Tex didn't understand what she was babbling about, and frankly the message was too complicated to type out, we decided that grapes would have to do. So Tex stopped by the General Store and disappeared inside while we chatted with Kingman through the car window.

"So have you arrested that killer yet?" asked Kingman.

"Not yet," I said.

"I'm telling you it's the ex-girlfriend," he said. "James Fox threatened to tell her husband about them, and so she killed him. It's always that way."

"We don't even know if she has a husband," I said.

"Oh, she's bound to. Humans like to travel through life in pairs, Max."

"That, I know," I said. "But we don't know anything about this particular woman, so let's first identify her, shall we, before we start casting aspersions."

"I like asparagus," Grace announced. "It's very tasty."

"So where are you going with the kid?" asked Kingman.

"To visit her daycare," I said. "The woman who runs it has closed the place down for business, and since we figure she might be sick, Grace wants to pay her a visit and wish her well."

"And bring her grapes!" Grace added for good measure. "Though now I'm wondering if we shouldn't have bought her asparagus instead. It's supposed to be very nutritious."

"I like the sentiment," said Kingman. "But grapes are over-rated. If I were you, I'd buy her an Xbox. That way she can play games while she's convalescing."

But since Tex had returned, we had to cut our conversation short and return to the business at hand. Which was: find out what was going on with Chantal and wish her a speedy recovery in case she really was sick.

It didn't take Tex long to arrive at our destination, and so he parked across the street and turned to us. "Are you sure about this?" he asked. "I mean, we don't know what's going on with this woman. For all we know, her husband might have died, or her mom or dad or something. And then we show up with a bag of grapes…" He shrugged. "It might send the wrong message."

"Grapes can never send a wrong message," Grace insisted stubbornly. "She's a very nice person, granddad, and she's always been nothing but kind to me, so I want her to know that I'm thinking of her and want her to get well soon."

We didn't write all that down on the tablet, but I think Tex understood, for he smiled and said, "Okay, let's just go and say hi, shall we?"

He let us out of the car, hoisted Grace up on his arm, and then we crossed the road. The daycare was located in a rather large villa and according to Grace, offered plenty of space to the toddlers in Chantal's care.

"You know what's odd?" said Dooley as Tex glanced in through the window to see if anybody was home. "That Tex doesn't know what's wrong with Chantal. I mean, he's a doctor, right? So if Chantal was sick, he would know."

"If she's one of his patients," I pointed out. "Which we don't know if she is."

Tex had pressed his finger to the doorbell, and we waited patiently. Suddenly, a window was opened over our heads, and a man yelled, "The daycare is closed, sir. So we can't take your daughter, I'm afraid."

"Oh, but she isn't… Why are you closed?"

"Family circumstances," said the man curtly.

"My name is Tex Poole," said Tex. "And I'm a doctor. This is Grace, my granddaughter, and we had actually heard that something happened to Chantal, so we wanted to drop off these." He held up the bag of grapes. "And to wish her well and thank her for taking such good care of Grace."

The man took in the grapes and seemed to like what he saw, for he said, "One sec." And then his head disappeared again, like a shy turtle reeling it in.

"I think it's the grapes that did the trick," Tex said. "Good thinking, Grace."

"You're welcome, granddad." She turned to us. "That man didn't look very nice. I just hope nothing has happened to Chantal. I mean, something bad."

"Why? Who is that man?"

"I have no idea. I've never seen him before."

"Maybe Chantal's brother who has come home from Mexico to take care of his sister," Dooley opined.

"Mexico?" I asked. "Why Mexico?"

"No reason. Just that he looked Mexican."

"More like Canadian," Grace said.

But before we could thresh this thing out properly and decide whether the man was Mexican or Canadian—two vastly different countries, to be sure—the man had opened the door and asked us to step in. We did as suggested and

NIC SAINT

found ourselves in the large daycare where Grace spent her days. It was a very pleasant and brightly decorated area with lots of corners where the kids could play and plenty of large boxes filled, no doubt, with toys.

"That's where I sleep!" said Grace, pointing to a couple of bunk beds in the corner of the large open space. "And that's where we eat!" she said. All in all, it was definitely a pleasant place to be, and now I could see why she liked to go there so much, especially if it was filled with all of her friends.

The man took the bag with the grapes from Tex and shook the doctor's hand. "Do you know that you're the first person to drop by? Chantal will be very pleased to hear it." He bent down to tickle Grace on the cheek. "Aren't you the cutest?"

But Grace didn't return the compliment. Instead, she said, "And aren't you the ugliest!"

"Grace!" I said with a laugh. "You can't say that kind of thing!"

"Why not? He is very ugly."

It was true that the man wasn't exactly the picture of beauty. He had a cut across his forehead where presumably someone had tested out the sharpness of a knife at one time, something strange was going on with his upper lip, where presumably that same knife had lingered, and his skin was red and puffy.

"Real beauty is on the inside, Grace," said Dooley.

Grace frowned at this. "I can't see his insides, but I can't imagine they're more beautiful than his outsides."

"So what's wrong with Chantal?" asked Tex, adopting his doctor's voice.

The man immediately responded, as people often do in the presence of a medical professional, by giving him a look of concern. "My sister was attacked in the street last night. She was just returning from her yoga class when someone yanked open her door at the red light and forced her to leave the vehicle. When she didn't immediately respond, the guy dragged her out and then took off in the car, also taking her purse with him, containing all of her money, ID, and credit cards. And since she took a nasty tumble, she managed to twist her ankle in the process and also hit her head on a concrete divider. She's been in the hospital all night, but the doctor said she's better off convalescing at home."

"I'm so sorry to hear it," said Tex. "Where was this?"

"Near the marina," said the man. "I'm Barry, by the way. Barry Ellis. Chantal's brother."

"And this happened last night?"

"Yeah, around ten o'clock. The yoga center is in one of those new buildings they put up by the marina, and Chantal has been going there for months without any problems. In fact, we thought it was a pretty safe area. Just goes to show you how wrong you can be."

"A carjacking, huh? And did you report it to the police?"

"Yeah, an officer came to the hospital to take my sister's statement. They said they were going to check the CCTV since the place is crawling with cameras, apparently."

Tex nodded. "My brother-in-law is the Chief of Police. If you'd like, I'll tell him to follow this up personally."

"Oh, would you do that?"

"Of course. Chantal has been taking such great care of my granddaughter. It's our turn to do something for her."

"Would you... would you like to see her?"

"Sure. And I'm sure Grace would love that. Wouldn't you, honey?"

"Oh, yes!" Grace said, much relieved that she would be seeing her beloved daycare mom.

Barry took us up the stairs and gently knocked on a bedroom door. "Sis? There's someone here to see you." He entered and ushered us into a bedroom, where Chantal was laid up in bed, looking a little bedraggled. Her head was all bandaged up, and her leg was in a cast. Now I understood why she wouldn't be able to take care of any kids for a while. But when she caught sight of Grace, her face morphed into an expression of sheer delight. "Gracie!" she cried, and immediately Grace ran over to the bed and gave the woman a big hug.

"This is Grace's grandfather," said Barry. "Doctor Poole."

"I know Doctor Poole," said Chantal with a grateful look at the man.

"So how are you?" asked the doctor and proceeded to listen intently as Chantal told him all about the injuries she had sustained. He also checked the medication she had been given. They earned his seal of approval, and he said that she should be up and about in no time. He assured her not to worry about her car because he would get in touch with Uncle Alec and ask him to fast-track any investigation that was ongoing in connection to Chantal's carjacking.

"I should have locked the door, I know," said Chantal. "But I don't always think about it. And this guy came from behind me, so I didn't see him coming."

"It's not your fault," Tex assured her. "And the police will get him for this."

"Thank you so much, Doctor Poole," she said. "And I'm sorry for standing you all up."

"That's all right. I've been babysitting Grace all morning, and we'll find a solution for tomorrow and the days after that."

Her face clouded. "Days? Are you sure?"

"It will take a little time before you can put weight on that ankle," he said. "And you might need some physiotherapy as well. But first, you need to get well again. If you like, I can check up with you, let's say in a day or two?"

"That would be amazing," said Chantal, deeply apprecia-
tive. "Thank you, Doctor."

"Don't mention it," said Tex with a kindly smile. "All part
of the service."

Grace gave the woman another hug, and then it was time
to say goodbye for the present. Barry led us out. "So you've
been taking care of your sister?" asked Tex as we stood in the
doorway.

"Yeah, her husband is away on business. He's been told
about what happened but is stuck in business meetings all
day today and tomorrow, so he couldn't immediately fly
back."

"Where is he?"

"Hong Kong. But he's arriving the day after tomorrow,
and then he'll take over. I live in Boston, but as soon as I
heard, I immediately came over here. I'll stay as long as
necessary. Chantal is the most amazing person I know, and
she deserves nothing less."

"That's very admirable of you," said Tex. "She's lucky to
have a brother like you, Barry."

"I'm lucky to have a sister like her," said Barry.

We said our goodbyes and got back into the car. On the
drive back home, Grace said, "I think I understand what you
meant by a person being beautiful on the inside even if he is
ugly on the outside, Dooley. Barry is definitely a beautiful
person for taking such good care of his sister. And I hope
Uncle Alec catches the guy that did this. Or you could catch
him, Max."

"Me!" I said.

"You are a detective, right?"

"Yes, but not that kind of detective."

"What kind are you then?"

"Well, I guess more the cerebral kind. Not the kind that

chases after car thieves and catches them and such. You need an action hero for that."

She smiled. "But you are an action hero, Max. You're my action hero."

Oh, dear. Not only did I have a killer to catch, dozens of caterpillars to herd, but now I also had to become an action hero and catch a carjacker? And all of that on absolutely no nap time at all, and with an empty litter box at home!

CHAPTER 15

*B*efore taking Grace home, Tex decided to drive us
into town and drop us off at the police station. He
had been in touch with his daughter and told her all about
the carjacking, and Odelia had asked him to bring us to the
station so we could join a meeting in her uncle's office to go
over the case. And so we found ourselves in the big man's
office, ensconced with the Chief, Odelia, and Chase, as they
discussed the ins and outs of this most baffling case of the
dead movie star.

"Okay, so according to the coroner's report," said Uncle
Alec as he read from his computer screen, "the cats were
right. The man did die from cyanide poisoning, enough of
which was found in his system to kill a dozen men."

"So he didn't drown?" asked Chase.

"No water in the lungs, so he was thrown into the pool
after he died."

"How was the cyanide administered?" asked Odelia.

"Traces of the poison were found in a can of Dr. Pepper in
Robert's cabin," said the Chief. "So most likely the stuff was

added to the soda, which was of the extra-sweet variety, to hide the taste of the cyanide. He drank the whole can."

"Yikes. Is it a painful death?" asked Chase.

"Well, it isn't pleasant," said Uncle Alec. "It prevents the body from processing oxygen, so sufferers will be gasping for breath, experiencing muscle spasms, and finally loss of consciousness. Death follows within minutes. Or at least that's what Abe told me. So." He placed his hands flat on his desk. "Talk to me about suspects."

Chase consulted his own notes. "We've interviewed the crew members, and they all tell the same story. Around the time of Ross's death, at ten o'clock this morning, the man was alone on the Aurora, having given his crew the morning off. Supposedly he was meeting someone, but nobody could tell us who."

"We checked CCTV covering the marina," said Odelia, picking up the story, "but we didn't see anybody arrive at the yacht. Not by car, taxi, or Uber. We did see the mass exodus of crew members from the vessel shortly before ten, but then nothing until I arrived around twelve. So for those two hours, nobody came anywhere near the boat."

"But that's impossible," said the Chief. "Surely the murderer must have boarded the vessel during that time."

"Unless he was already on the boat?" Chase suggested. "Though we should have seen him leave if that were the case."

"Unless he came and went by boat," Odelia pointed out. "He could have chartered a small boat or even used a dinghy—"

"Or swam."

"Or swam. In which case, the cameras wouldn't have picked him up."

"Doesn't the Aurora have its own CCTV system?" asked Uncle Alec.

"It does, but since Robert hated to be monitored or filmed, he invariably instructed the crew to turn it off, which they did. The only time the security cameras were activated was at night, to make sure the crew and passengers were secure. But in the morning, everything was switched off again. Unfortunately for us."

"And fortunately for the killer," Uncle Alec grunted unhappily. "Why install a state-of-the-art security system and then not use it? That doesn't make sense."

"Robert was very concerned about his privacy," Odelia explained. "He hated the thought of anyone filming him."

"Weird hang-up for an actor."

"Or maybe he was up to stuff that wasn't up to snuff?" Chase suggested.

"We did find a small baggie of pills stuffed behind the bed," said Odelia.

"Oh, yes," said Uncle Alec and put his reading glasses back on his nose. "Toxicological analysis of the pills has revealed them as fentanyl. So apparently our Mr. Ross liked his candy."

"We also found an empty safe," said Chase. "And I mean literally empty. The door ajar and nothing inside. Which struck me as odd. We dusted the safe for prints but only found Ross's fingerprints."

"I wonder what was in that safe," said Uncle Alec. He turned to me for some reason. "Have your cats had a chance to interrogate the dog?"

"They did talk to the dog, didn't you, Max?" asked Odelia.

"We did," I confirmed. "But unfortunately, she was being taken for a walk around the time of the murder, so she couldn't tell us what happened."

"Ask her about the safe," said Odelia. "We need to know what was in it."

"Gotcha," I said, though I wasn't all that sanguine that the dog would talk. I had the impression she was one of those reticent dogs who don't like to share information about their owners. "Where is she right now?"

"Where is the dog?" asked Odelia.

"One of the crew members took her," said the Chief. "Robert's brother is flying in from France, where he lives. He'll handle the funeral arrangements and hopefully adopt the dog."

"Poor Flame," said Dooley. "To lose your human is one thing, but now she'll have to go and live with a complete stranger in a strange land far away."

"France isn't that strange," I said. "And maybe this brother is much nicer than Robert." Though I had the impression that the actor had been a lot kinder to his dog than he had been to his crew, which is often the way.

"Okay, so let's get back to possible suspects," said the Chief. "What have you got for me?"

"So the crew members all painted the same picture of Robert being a pretty obnoxious boss," said Chase. "Wouldn't allow the crew to look him in the eye, wanted them to be almost invisible while also serving him as if he was the emperor of China, and he had a penchant for flirting with female crew members and not taking no for an answer. He picked one favorite and then hounded her relentlessly. During this trip, he favored Susanne Palmer, who said the experience was traumatic. She was guarded as much as possible by her colleagues, and also by Captain Gerard, which must have caused Robert to become very frustrated indeed."

"Did any actual harassment take place?" asked the Chief with a note of concern.

"Not according to Suzanne. But I had the impression she wasn't telling us the full truth, so it's possible that something did happen she doesn't want to talk about. But the crew members have closed ranks, so it's impossible to know for sure what did or did not happen."

"Okay, so let's pencil this Suzanne Palmer in as a suspect," said the Chief. "Though she presumably left the ship along with the rest of the crew?"

"She did. She left the Aurora only to return after the body had already been found."

"She could always have come back via the water," said the Chief. "So let's put her on the list of suspects. Anyone else?"

"If something did happen to Suzanne, any other member of the crew might have felt compelled to take revenge," said Odelia. "Though the person closest to Suzanne appears to have been Jeanine Bishop. According to the others, those two are best friends and spent a lot of time together."

"The captain also seemed very protective of Suzanne," said Chase. "So if Robert did try something with Suzanne, Gerard might have decided to take matters into his own hands to protect her from further harm."

"Okay, so basically the entire crew are all suspects," said the Chief.

"Except maybe for Marcus O'Reilly," said Odelia. "Who seems to have been universally despised by his colleagues. But very well-liked by Ross himself."

"Anyone else? What about this Sebastian Poe I keep hearing about?"

"I did some checking on the guy," said Chase, "and Sebastian Poe seems to have disappeared a couple of weeks ago. He lived in Miami with his girlfriend, and one day he left home and never returned. Police tracked his movements and came as far as Sunset Harbour, where Poe had a boat. He took off one morning, and that's where the trail ends. Before he left, he told his girlfriend he was meeting a client that day —Poe was a real estate broker for a luxury property realtor— but according to his personal assistant, he had cleared his calendar and had no meetings scheduled for that day or the next."

"But according to the dog, Poe suddenly turned up on the Aurora?" asked the Chief.

"That's what Flame claims," said Odelia, glancing in my direction.

"Funny name, Flame," said her uncle with a grin. But then he became serious again. "So what's the story with this Poe?"

"Best friends with Robert," said Chase, "and they kept in touch, meeting up from time to time and spending holidays together. From what I could glean, they were both cut from the same cloth: confirmed bachelors who enjoyed chasing women and liked life in the fast lane, though Poe had been with his girlfriend for some time. There was even talk of marriage."

"Okay, so let's follow up on this disappearance story," said the Chief. "Check where the Aurora was when Poe went missing. Maybe he met up with his friend, and something happened. So next, we have…" He frowned at his screen. "Jane Collins?"

"That's right. By all accounts, Robert and Jane were high school sweethearts. But then, for some reason, they broke up, Robert left town, and Jane ended up marrying Bert Collins. I've already arranged for an interview with Mr. and Mrs. Collins, Chief."

"Could she be our mystery guest?" asked Uncle Alec.

"It's possible," said Odelia. "The man returns to Hampton Cove after twenty-five years, so it wouldn't surprise me if he wanted to meet his former girlfriend and talk about old times. Though if he did, she never showed up."

"Or maybe she did," said the Chief, arching a meaningful, bushy brow. As we all made to leave his office, Uncle Alec halted us in our tracks. "So what's all this I hear about my mother running amok in Hampton Cove?"

Odelia gave him a shame-faced look. "I'm afraid that's my fault, Uncle Alec. Gran was all over the crime scene, so in an attempt to make her do something useful, I asked her to talk to the people in town about Ross. You know, what they thought about him and what kind of a person he was. But instead, she's gone and interviewed the woman who runs the awards committee for the Chamber of Commerce and roped in Scarlett to run a parallel investigation as members of their neighborhood watch."

Uncle Alec groaned and grabbed at the few remaining strands of hair on his scalp that had survived the attrition. "Not again with this neighborhood watch! I thought they were all done with that nonsense!"

"Apparently not. They're going door to door to talk to people."

"Which maybe isn't such a bad thing?" Chase suggested carefully. "We're understaffed as it is, Chief, so if they can find out what people thought of Ross or what he's been up to since the Aurora moored here, what places he visited, and the kind of people he saw, it could help our investigation?"

"Yeah, but she's actually arresting people," said the Chief. "Or at least that's what this woman, this Caroline Poots claims. And all because she decided to give the guy an award. As if giving an actor an award is some kind of crime!"

"I'll talk to her," Odelia assured her uncle. "Tell her to take it easy on the arresting people stuff."

"You do that. And tell her that if she doesn't calm down, I'll arrest her!"

"Oh, there was one other thing," said Odelia. "My dad talked to Grace's daycare owner. Chantal Jones was the victim of a carjacking last night. After she finished her yoga class, someone dragged her from her car and took off in it. She suffered a sprained ankle and a concussion."

"Did she report it?"

"She did, and she said it happened at ten o'clock last night near the marina."

"And you think there's a connection with the Ross case?"

Odelia shrugged. "Might be worth looking into?"

"Check with the officer in charge of the carjacking," her uncle instructed. "There might be something in it. And now let's get cracking, people. Chop chop. And that goes for you, too, Max and Dooley," he added with a slight grin.

Dooley turned to me. "What about our litter, Max? We probably should mention the litter monster to the Chief so he can look into that, too."

"Maybe now is not the time, Dooley," I told my friend.

"But what if Flame is the litter monster, Max? This could all be connected!"

"I doubt it, buddy," I said.

And anyway, somehow I had a feeling that Uncle Alec wouldn't be all that interested in discovering who had stolen our litter that morning. The big man had more important things to deal with at the moment. Like finding a killer.

CHAPTER 16

$\mathcal{O}$ delia and Chase first decided to drop in on the officer handling the Chantal Jones carjacking case. Sarah Flunk, a fine-boned, freckle-faced young officer with glorious red hair, was studying something on her computer when we approached her. She glanced down at us and frowned, as if wondering what a pair of cats were doing in the police precinct. And for a moment, I thought she would assume we had been placed under arrest and escort us to interview room number one for interrogation. But then I realized that her frown wasn't meant for us but simply a consequence of her thought process, as her next words made clear.

"I don't get it, Chase. I've been going over the marina CCTV footage from last night, and it's almost as if the carjacker knew where all the cameras were located."

She turned her computer, and we all looked intently at Sarah's screen, where we were treated to not-very-clear images of the events as Chantal had already described them to us. And it was exactly as she had outlined: the moment she stopped at a red light, the carjacker had snuck up to her,

99

yanked open her car door, and dragged her out of the car, then jumped into the car and raced off at a great rate of speed while Chantal lay on the ground, seemingly unconscious after having knocked her head on a concrete divider.

"Is she going to be all right?" asked Odelia with concern.

"She sustained a nasty bump to the head, but when I spoke with her, she seemed to be doing fine. Very concerned about the daycare, since under no circumstances can she take care of any kids at the moment."

"I know. She's our daughter's daycare provider," Odelia explained. "My dad paid her a visit, and he said she mostly seemed shaken by what happened."

"I can only imagine," said Sarah. "To be suddenly confronted by this maniac." She had blown up the images, but the resolution wasn't all that great. And definitely not sufficient to positively ID the perpetrator or even to determine whether it was a he or a she. And on top of that, he kept his face turned away from the camera at all times. "See what I mean? Almost as if he knows where the camera is. Though I'm pretty sure it's a guy."

The man was dressed in a hoodie, jeans, and sneakers, and from the way he moved, it seemed plausible that he would be of the male persuasion.

"Did you follow the car on other cameras?"

"I did, and I got it as far as Marlin Road, but then it enters a CCTV dead zone and disappears. I haven't been able to pick it up after that. Though I've put out an APB on the stolen vehicle. Maybe if we're lucky, we'll find it."

"What do you think, Chase?" asked Odelia. "Any connection with the Ross case?"

"Apart from the fact that it happened at the marina, I'm not sure," Chase confessed.

"Did anything happen on the Aurora last night around ten?" asked Sarah.

"Not that we know of," said Chase. "But we'll ask Captain Gerard. We're going to see him now, and hopefully this time he'll give us something more to work with. So far, all of the crew members have been pretty reticent."

"Yeah, that's my impression also," said Odelia. "Almost as if they're all hiding something."

"Good work, Sarah," said Chase. "Let me know when you find that car."

"Will do, boss," said the officer.

Our next stop was at the Hampton Cove Springs Hotel, where the crew of the Aurora were being put up for the time being until the investigation was concluded and they could all go home. The company that employed them paid for their stay there, and even though it wasn't exactly a five-star hotel, it was still a fine place. Located near the marina, it was conveniently close to the Aurora, so the moment the yacht had been cleared, they could board. But for now, they were all forced to stay put, and clearly they weren't happy about it. At least if Captain Gerard's first words were anything to go by.

"How long are you planning to keep us here?" the gray-haired captain asked.

We were seated in the hotel bar, where the captain had already been having a modest party, judging by the array of glasses on the table.

"Until the crime scene people release the yacht and the investigation is concluded," said Chase.

"But that could take weeks!"

"I'm sure it won't take that long," Chase assured him. "Now we would like to ask you a few more questions, Mr. Gerard."

"Of course you do," said the captain moodily. "Questions, questions, questions, and never any answers. That's the way it goes."

"So what can you tell us about the safe in Mr. Ross's suite, sir?"

"Nothing," said the captain with a touch of belligerence.

"The safe was found empty," Chase clarified.

"What makes you think there was ever anything inside that safe to begin with?"

"We have reason to believe that Mr. Ross kept his fentanyl pills in that safe. So what can you tell us about that?"

The man lapsed into silence for a moment, then gave the detective a cautious look. "Who told you?"

"We have our sources," Chase said stoically.

The captain sighed and took another swig from his drink. He didn't look as neatly attired and groomed as he had done earlier that day. "Okay, fine. So Ross did keep his pills in that safe, you're absolutely right about that. And he also kept his cash in there, and lots of it."

"Cash and pills?"

"And other substances," said the captain reluctantly.

"What substances?"

"Cocaine, mainly. The man was an addict, pure and simple. Couldn't keep his nose out of the stuff. Basically, he couldn't get through the day without it."

"And the cash?"

"To buy his stash, or what do you think?"

"Where did he get this stash?"

The captain shrugged. "He had contacts. Dealers in every port, so to speak. These days everything is done online, detective, but then I probably don't have to tell you that. You have your contacts on your phone, and then when you need something, you simply set up a delivery."

"So how did that work, exactly? Did he send a crew member, or did he handle everything himself?"

"Mostly he would send a crew member. He didn't like to

get involved in the tawdry business of meeting drug dealers in the ports we visited."

"Who?"

The captain's lips thinned, but finally, he said, "Marcus. He was the only one Ross trusted enough with the money to handle his drug deals for him."

"According to most crew members we spoke with, Marcus was also the least popular member," said Odelia. "Is that because he handled Ross's drug deals?"

"That probably was part of it, yeah," said the captain. "But Marcus is simply a very unpleasant human being. Like Ross, he could be very manipulative and disagreeable towards women, so they pretty much banded together and protected each other from his frequent attempts to hook up with them. And then of course, he wasn't averse to the occasional snort himself."

"Ross and Marcus got high together?"

"I wouldn't go that far. As I told you this morning, Ross wasn't the kind of person who liked to fraternize with the crew, and that included Marcus. But he did share some of his stash with him from time to time, mainly to keep him quiet in case there was trouble, and also because the man was stingy. So instead of paying him outright for his services as a courier, he paid him in pills and coke and booze."

"And Marcus was happy with this arrangement?"

"Happy as a clam. He also claimed that Ross was going to get him a part in his next movie. He had high hopes, that one, and couldn't stop annoying his colleagues with his tall tales about being the next Fox villain and becoming a major star in his own right. Though I think we all saw through it and figured Ross was simply feeding him this stuff to keep him happy."

Odelia and Chase shared a look, and I could tell what they were thinking. What if Marcus had discovered that all of Ross's promises had been nothing but lies? That he never intended to cast him in any of his movies? Marcus wouldn't have been happy about that, to say the least.

"Okay, so let's talk about Suzanne Palmer," Odelia suggested.

"What do you want to know?" asked the captain wearily.

"Suzanne has told us that Ross kept making lewd comments to her and trying to persuade her to spend the night in his suite. She also said that nothing ever happened and that she managed to turn him down every time."

"But we think that something did happen," Chase added. "A man like Ross would never take no for an answer."

They both stared expectantly at the captain, who shrugged his shoulders. "You'll have to ask Suzanne. Frankly, I have nothing more to say about that."

"You're the captain, Mr. Gerard," Chase pointed out. "If something did happen, you would know all about it."

"Stuff happens on a ship that even the captain doesn't know about. Like I said, if you want to know what happened between Ross and Suzanne, you'll have to talk to her."

"So something did happen," said Chase.

But Captain Gerard wasn't budging on this one. So Odelia leaned forward. "She can still file a complaint, you know. Even though the man is dead, it's not too late to come forward and tell us what happened. He can't engage any of his fancy lawyers now. So maybe this is the time to tell us the truth."

He stared at his drink for a long time, swirling its contents as he pursed his lips. "Look, I gave Suzanne my word I wouldn't tell anyone," he said finally. "And I'm a man of my word. But if you really want to know what happened, I suggest you talk to Jeanine Bishop. She's Suzanne's best friend. So if anything did happen, Suzanne would have told her, not me."

The inference was clear enough. Suzanne wouldn't have confided in anyone other than her friend Jeanine. But at least now we knew that Ross had seriously misbehaved, which gave Suzanne a strong motive to have killed the man.

"One more question, sir," said Odelia. "Did something happen on the Aurora last night before or around ten o'clock? Some trouble with one of Mr. Ross's drug dealers, perhaps?"

The captain frowned. "I wouldn't know, as I decided to have an early night and went to bed at nine."

"And you didn't hear from the other crew members about some altercation?"

He shook his head. "Nothing happened as far as I know."

"Thank you, captain," said Chase, getting up. But then as we walked away, he turned. "One more thing. Does the name Sebastian Poe ring a bell?"

The look of sheer panic on the man's face told us all we needed to know.

CHAPTER 17

"Okay, I guess I probably should have told you this sooner," said the captain. His drink had been topped up, and after he had quaffed deeply and greedily, he seemed ready to spill the beans. "Sebastian Poe was one of Ross's best friends. Rumor had it they went to school together. I'm not sure if that's true, but what is true is that they were thick as thieves. Occasionally, Poe would board the Aurora for an all-weekend binge with his good friend Ross, which would mostly include a lot of booze, a lot of drugs, and a lot of women. Sometimes others would join them, and the end result would be forty-eight or seventy-two hours of debauchery. It wasn't a lot of fun for the crew, but we got paid handsomely to keep our mouths shut and to keep the booze and the food coming. Mostly, these parties would be organized far away from shore, so no nosy parkers would be any the wiser, and no paparazzi could snap embarrassing pictures to be sold to the tabloids, compromising all involved."

"So that's where that stash of cash came in," said Chase. "To pay for all of this."

The captain nodded. "I'm not proud of it, but it was true that the man was a great tipper. And also, we knew what we were getting into when we signed up. Ross had a reputation with the yacht company."

"And they didn't mind?"

The captain looked mildly embarrassed. "The man was a bona fide millionaire, detective. And when enough money changes hands, it's amazing what an effect that can have on a guilty conscience. And if someone did complain, they were quickly bought off and sent packing."

"So what happened with Sebastian Poe?"

"Okay, so Ross had told us about another one of his weekends he wanted to organize. This time we were in the Bahamas, a safe distance from Bimini, the nearest island, and the only guest was Poe, along with some local women Marcus had managed to wrangle up and deliver to the Aurora. Poe arrived on his own boat, and before long, the party was in full swing. By the time I decided to turn in for the night, they were having a ball. Loud music, dancing, you know the drill. So I plugged in my earplugs and went to bed. Marcus woke me up. He said something terrible had happened. So I followed him to the main deck, and we found Ross there, blood all over him, completely out of it. The women sat huddled to one side, looking scared out of their wits. And of Poe, there was no trace, even though his boat was still there."

"So what happened?"

"No idea," said the captain. "Ross was wasted and couldn't tell us anything, and if the girls knew, they weren't talking, afraid we'd call the cops."

"So why didn't you call the cops?"

He heaved a deep sigh. "Can you imagine the scandal? Not only would Ross's life have been over, but ours as well, and those women. So Marcus ferried them back to the island,

and we tried to clean up Ross as well as we could, and also the deck and the guy's suite, which was a mess. We chucked everything overboard—the booze, the drugs, the pills—and tucked our charge into bed to sleep off his bender, hoping he'd be able to tell us what happened in the morning. Only the next day, it was obvious he had no clue. He even asked about Poe, wanting to know where he'd gone off to. But then later, when Marcus finally returned from his trip, he said that one of the women told him that there had been a fight. Apparently, Ross and Poe had fallen out, both drunk as skunks, and had started slugging away at each other. Ross had aimed a bottle at his friend's head, which had hit its target, and Poe had fallen overboard. One of the women had even gone in but hadn't been able to find the guy. So, in all likelihood, he drowned."

"So Ross killed his best friend, and nobody talked?"

"That's pretty much the gist of it," the captain admitted. "Though at the time, we decided that it must have been a tragic accident. Ross didn't want to kill Poe, but it happened anyway."

"I don't believe this."

"We got together, the entire crew, in the mess, and talked things through. The crew members who had served at the party swore up and down they hadn't been present when the altercation took place, since Ross had basically told them to leave. So the only witnesses were Ross himself, who couldn't remember a thing, and the prostitutes. And they certainly weren't going to talk. So basically, we had to decide if we wanted to involve the police or not. Ross had already told us not to and threatened us with untold consequences if we did, and we knew he had the power to make good on his threat. He had also promised us a big payday if we kept our mouths shut. So in the end, we put it to a vote, and the majority decided to pretend the incident never happened. Poe's boat was cut loose, and that was the end of that."

"Incredible," said Chase, shaking his head.

"Until last night," said the captain.

"Last night? So something did happen last night?"

He nodded, took another big gulp from his drink, and said, "Poe showed up."

"Poe showed up? The dead man?"

"Apparently, he didn't die. It gave us all quite a fright, I have to say. And it freaked Ross out big time. Out of the blue, Sebastian Poe suddenly turned up and told his old friend that he had another thing coming if he thought he could get away with murder. Which is when Ross invited Poe into his suite and locked the door. So unfortunately, I have no way of knowing what was said. All I know is that one hour later, Poe suddenly left, walked off the boat, and disappeared."

"What time was this?" asked Odelia.

"Around ten o'clock. I also have to say he didn't look well. Even though we all recognized him, and so did Ross, he looked as if he'd been living under a rock for the past couple of weeks. He'd grown a beard, and his skin was blotchy, and there was this weird look in his eyes, almost as if he'd gone feral."

"Did you ask Ross about it?"

"Of course. But he said nothing happened, and Poe was never on the boat. But I have to say he looked pretty spooked. Almost like he'd seen a ghost."

"Which he had," Chase pointed out.

"What did the others say?"

"I think they were all relieved that Poe didn't die. Even though we had put the matter to a vote, none of us felt happy about the decision to pretend that the incident didn't take place. I mean, it's one thing to ignore the booze and the dope, but another to brush murder under the carpet in exchange for money."

"How much did Ross pay so you would all keep quiet?"

"A hundred thousand each. In cash. And he was true to his word."

"So you're all a hundred thousand richer? That explains why his safe was empty."

"Oh, there was plenty left in that famous safe of his. And before you ask, no, I didn't clean it out. I don't know who did."

"Who had access to that safe?"

He gave us a meaningful look. "As far as I can tell, only Marcus did."

"When did this incident with Poe take place?" asked Odelia.

"Six weeks ago."

"Poe must have drifted ashore on one of the islands," said Chase. "Where he managed to survive, or maybe he was saved by the locals who took him in and nursed him back to health."

"Like I said, the man looked terrible. And I had the impression he wasn't all there either."

"Could he have returned the next day to kill his former best friend?"

"Your guess is as good as mine. Though I'd say there's a good chance he did. If your best friend knocks you off your boat and leaves you to drown, I don't think you'd be happy about it."

CHAPTER 18

"*R*obert Ross was not a very nice man, Max," said Dooley as we left Captain Gerard drowning his sorrows at the bar.

"No, he wasn't," I confirmed.

"Though of course, if you're a spy who has to save the world, you probably can't always be the nice guy. When you're faced with a criminal mastermind like Dr. Maybe, you can't play nice. You have to be tough."

"Ross was an actor playing a part, Dooley," I pointed out. "He wasn't an actual spy tasked with saving the world."

"Oh, I know, Max, but still. An actor of his caliber must have had a hard time shaking the role he played once the cameras stopped filming. It's all about immersing yourself, Max."

"Don't tell me. You saw a documentary?"

"How did you know? It was all about method acting and how some actors will go to extreme lengths to prepare for a certain part. Like losing a lot of weight or gaining a lot of pounds. So maybe Ross had become so identified with his role as James Fox that he couldn't differentiate between Ross and Fox. As if they were one and the same person."

"James Fox wouldn't throw boozy parties on his private yacht and then kill his friend," I said.

"Unless he had just discovered that this friend was, in actual fact, an agent for Dr. Maybe!" said Dooley. "And I think we need to look into this Poe guy and see if he isn't secretly the leader of a global criminal cabal, Max."

I sighed. "Oh, Dooley."

We had arrived at the door where, according to Chase's information, Marcus O'Reilly was staying. The man opened the door, looking a little bedraggled. He was dressed in boxer shorts and a stained tank top and stared at us as if he'd never seen us before. Then his face cleared. "Detective Kingsley! Come on in. Can I offer you something to drink? Or milk for your cats?"

"No, we're fine," said Chase as we entered the room. The room looked as untidy as the man himself, with clothes strewn about and a suitcase open on the bed. He clearly hadn't finished unpacking yet, or maybe he didn't intend to. After all, once the investigation was concluded, all these people were free to return to the Aurora, presumably to sail her back to her home port.

"We would like to ask you a few more questions, Mr. O'Reilly," said Odelia as she looked for a place to sit. When nothing seemed convenient, she decided to remain standing, which was probably a good idea.

"Shoot," said the guy who had been Ross's consigliere if Captain Gerard's words were to be believed, or at least his secret drug supplier.

"I would like to tell you a story," said Chase, causing me and Dooley to look up in surprise.

"I didn't know Chase was into storytelling," Dooley confessed.

"Me neither," I said.

"I hope it will be a fun story. I love a good story, Max."

"So there was a millionaire actor who rented a private yacht to go sailing in the Bahamas. Only he loved to throw private parties on his boat, and during one of those parties, he accidentally hit his best friend on the head. The friend fell overboard and seemingly drowned. At which point the crew decided to hold a meeting to decide whether to report the incident to the police or not. The majority won the vote, and the incident was hushed up, in exchange for a hundred thousand in cash from the actor to every member of the crew."

The man had blanched considerably and now dropped down on the bed, his legs not able to carry his weight anymore.

"But then suddenly last night, the dead man rose from the dead and showed up on the yacht, surprising everyone, and most of all the actor. Now, I don't know what was said, but I would sure love to know. Maybe the actor cleaned out his safe and paid off his friend, earning his silence. Or maybe he gave him a part of his personal stash of drugs. For the actor was also secretly or not-so-secretly addicted to opioids and cocaine, and he paid a member of his crew to ferry back and forth between the boat and the islands they passed to supply him with enough of both to stun an elephant. Does any of this ring a bell, Mr. O'Reilly?"

The guy swallowed once or twice. "How—how do you know all this?"

"That's not important," said Chase. "What is important is the role that you played. So, is it true that you were Mr. Ross's drug runner?"

The guy nodded. "I guess so. He needed someone to get his stuff for him, and for some reason, he chose me."

"And rewarded you with part of his stash."

"I'm not an addict if that's what you're suggesting," said

the man. "I never touched the stuff myself, but it's true that he did, and in copious quantities too. I guess you could say that he was a very sick man."

"And yet you kept supplying him with the stuff that was most likely going to kill him and almost killed his friend Sebastian Poe."

"I wasn't there when that happened. None of us were."

"So, I'm going to put it to you straight, Mr. O'Reilly," said Chase. "And I want you to give me an honest answer this time, all right?"

The man nodded fervently.

"Did you clear out Mr. Ross's safe this morning?"

"No, I did not."

"Second question, and think carefully before you respond. To your knowledge, did Mr. Ross ever assault Miss Palmer?"

"Yeah, he did. Or at least that's what she claimed. There were no witnesses, apart from her and Ross, but apparently, he made a move on her and she had to fight him off. And since he wouldn't take no for an answer, she conked him."

"Conked him?"

"With his Golden Globe Award. Left a nasty bruise on his head and broke the skin. I know because it was me that had to dress the cut later on. He wouldn't shut up about what a horrible person Suzanne was, though he used much stronger language than that."

"So why didn't he fire her from the crew?"

"He couldn't. Not after what he did to Poe. We pretty much had the guy over a barrel. Though of course he also had us over the same barrel since we probably should have notified the authorities when Poe went overboard. And instead, we cut his boat loose and pretended nothing happened."

"There's nothing probably about it," said Chase. "Your employer murdered a man, and you decided to cover it up."

"Poe didn't die," said Marcus feebly. "Somehow he survived."

"You didn't know that."

"So what happened last night?" asked Odelia. "Between Ross and Poe?"

Marcus shook his head. "I have no idea. Though probably nothing good. When Poe finally came storming out of Ross's suite, he looked like a man with murder on his mind."

"So do you think he returned the next morning to take revenge on his old friend?"

Marcus shrugged helplessly. "From what I saw of Poe last night, I'd say that's extremely likely."

"Ross didn't discuss it with you? Or the incident where Mr. Poe went overboard?"

"Never. After he paid us for our silence, he never mentioned it again. Though I could tell it haunted his dreams. He never organized a party again, and he became strangely subdued, as if the guilt was eating away at him."

"Or maybe he was afraid someone would talk and he'd be arrested."

"I did once see him check news sites about Poe's disappearance, so it definitely kept him up at night. But like I said, he never mentioned it again."

"And the authorities never contacted him to ask about Poe suddenly going missing?"

"Not to my knowledge. According to the papers, they figured Poe and his girlfriend had fallen out. Neighbors had heard screaming and shouting only the day before, so they suspected her of foul play, but nothing was ever proven."

"Apparently, the girlfriend had connections with organized crime," Chase told Odelia. "Which is why the police figured her family had 'fixed' Poe."

"Another reason Ross was so nervous about what happened. If Poe's girlfriend's family found out about what really happened, they might have come after him."

"Maybe they did," Chase pointed out. "If Poe was alive, he could have told his girlfriend, and if she told her family, they could have decided to get even."

"What a story," said Dooley with a touch of breathless-ness. "It's not Snow White and the Seven Dwarfs, but it's still very gripping, isn't it, Max?"

"It is," I said.

"Maybe Disney will make a movie about it!"

"Somehow I doubt it. It's not all that suitable for kids, wouldn't you say?"

"No, I guess you're right. It doesn't have that wholesome quality."

More like a decidedly unwholesome quality.

CHAPTER 19

The next door we knocked on was Suzanne Palmer's door. Only when she opened and we stepped in, we found that she wasn't alone but in the presence of Jeanine Bishop.

"We would like to make a statement," Suzanne announced, tilting her chin. "And we would like to do it together."

"Captain Gerard told us that you talked to him," Jeanine explained.

"Then he also told you that we know what happened on the Aurora?" said Odelia. She had adopted a kindly tone, as she often does. She clearly felt for the woman who had been forced to bear the brunt of Mr. Ross's ill-conceived and unwelcome advances.

Suzanne nodded. Tears had formed in her eyes, and Jeanine now took her hand in support. "Robert Ross was an evil man," Suzanne announced. "And I know I probably should have said something sooner, and the fact that I didn't will probably haunt me forever, but... He attacked me. I fended him off and managed to get him away from me, but if

I hadn't succeeded..." Her voice broke, and it was obvious that the incident had made a powerful impression on her.

"You hit him over the head with his Golden Globe, is that correct?" asked Chase.

Suzanne nodded. "He needed stitches, so Captain Gerard headed straight to the nearest port where he received medical attention."

"I thought Marcus O'Reilly patched him up?"

"Marcus isn't a trained nurse, detective," said Jeanine. "Like you said, he patched him up to the best of his abilities, but when Ross inspected his handiwork in the mirror, he had a meltdown. Claimed he would never work again with the kind of scar Marcus's needlework would leave and demanded to be taken to a hospital immediately. So Gerard did as he was told, though I have to say Marcus probably did a better job than the nurse at the hospital did."

"At least I didn't have to come anywhere near the man again," said Suzanne with a faint smile at the recollection.

"I served him from that moment on," said Jeanine, "with Suzanne being relegated to galley duties. Which was a good thing for all involved."

"And he didn't try anything funny with you?" asked Chase.

"No, he didn't. Said I wasn't his type and kept complaining about his scar, which got inflamed at some point and gave him a lot of grief."

"Those Golden Globes are pretty solid," said Suzanne.

"Well, I just think it served him right. The man was a very unpleasant character. Possibly the most unpleasant client I've ever worked for, and I've been doing this job for almost twenty years now. Though we once worked for a family with kids, and they were also pretty awful. Both the parents and the kids."

"Oh, imagine Ross having kids," said Suzanne. "The

horror."

"What can you tell us about Sebastian Poe?" asked Odelia.

And so the two women told us all about Mr. Poe, though their account didn't add anything more to the story than we already knew, unfortunately. They also thought that Poe just might be Ross's killer but couldn't be sure.

"For what it's worth, detective," said Suzanne, "I, for one, feel very sorry for what we did to that poor man. I was one of the few people who voted in favor of going to the police, but I was overruled by the majority."

"I also voted in favor," said Jeanine. "And maybe we should have gone to the police anyway, though the others would probably have denied everything, and Ross certainly would have."

"He said that if we talked, we'd never work in the hospitality industry again," said Suzanne. "And I could live with that. After working on the Aurora, I wanted to quit anyway."

"So what are you going to do now?" asked Odelia.

"Oh, I don't know. Return home and stay with my parents for a while. Think about what I'll do next. Or maybe I could join my mom. She runs a diner in my home town and has always expressed a fervent wish that I would join her one day. I could waitress while she does the kitchen. My grandmother also works there, so it's pretty much a family affair. And to be honest, nothing would suit me better right now than to be home again and spend time with my family."

We left them to discuss their respective futures, and as Odelia closed the door, she said, "I'm starting to suspect more and more that the man who carjacked Chantal Jones's car last night just might have been Sebastian Poe."

"But why?" asked Chase. "If he managed to get from his island all the way to Hampton Cove, don't you think he would have had transport?"

"I don't know, but I think it's imperative that we find him.

He could very well be our killer."

"I think the case is closed already, Max," said Dooley as we returned to the lobby of the hotel. "Sebastian Poe is obviously the killer. He was knocked off the Aurora, ended up on some remote island where he was nursed back to health by locals, and once his memory returned, he set out to take revenge on his former best friend who tried to kill him. In fact..." He gave me a look of significance. "I think I may know Mr. Poe's real name."

"What is it?" I asked.

"Jason Bourne, of course! Left out at sea to die, with no recollection of who he is or what he's done, once his body is healed by a beautiful woman—"

"I think it was an elderly fisherman."

"—he discovers his true identity and goes in search of the people who did this to him. Sebastian Poe is Jason Bourne, Max!"

"Somehow I doubt it, Dooley."

"And of course, he killed Robert Ross." He gasped and held a paw to his face. "Max!"

"What?"

"He's not done!"

"He isn't?"

"Of course not! He'll want revenge on all the people he holds responsible for what happened to him. Next, he'll go after the crew members, finishing them off one by one. And then when he's done with them, he'll start on those women from the island who were there that night. There will be a lot of dead bodies before this history is done, Max."

"I don't think so."

"Of course there will be. There's Jason Bourne 1, 2, 3, and 4, and there are spin-offs, Max. And we all know that spin-offs are always a lot worse than the original."

Oh, dear Lord.

CHAPTER 20

*I*t had taken the neighborhood watch, in its new guise as a mixed cat and human collaboration, a little time to determine the identity of the mystery woman they assumed had paid a visit to Ross on his private yacht. And in the end, it was actually Harriet who had found her. After talking to several of their friends, Buster had remembered that Fido had a customer in his hair salon that morning who had remembered the actor with fondness. According to her, she had been his English teacher when he was in high school, and even then she had seen what a great talent he possessed.

"When he played King Lear, I knew he was destined for greatness," she told Fido, who responded that there certainly were Shakespearean elements hidden in the work of the author of the James Fox books, something the schoolteacher had wholeheartedly agreed with.

"James Fox *is* Shakespeare," she had claimed. "Only without the shooting and the high-tech gizmos, of course. But the themes and the general theatricality are definitely inspired by the Bard." She had clasped her hands together.

"Oh, and to think I was the one who discovered and nurtured his talent. What a gift to the world!"

"And such a loss," Fido had said fervently, for he was a huge fan of Robert Ross, as were most of the people who had passed through the salon that afternoon, all eager to find out the latest about the terrible murder that had rocked their community. It isn't every day that an A-list Hollywood star is murdered. And even more so when that major movie star was a local!

And that's when Buster dropped his bombshell. "So the schoolteacher also told Fido that Robert had been such a lovely boy, and that she had been so sad when he and Jane broke up."

This was the moment Harriet had perked up her ears. "Jane?"

"Yes, Jane Collins. Apparently, she and Robert were destined to be together forever, but unfortunately, it was not to be, and they soon broke up, and then Robert left town, never to return until today."

"Jane Collins," Harriet had repeated, as if in a daze. She had solved the murder! She knew it. She just knew it. Jane Collins had paid a visit to Robert Ross that morning, after not having seen the man for twenty-five years, and for some reason had carried along with her on her date a little vial of cyanide, which she had deposited in her former boyfriend's drink. But when Buster asked her why she would have done such a thing, she had to admit that as far as motive was concerned, things were still a little hazy.

"But I'll figure it out," she said. "Just you wait and see."

They had immediately returned to the Star Hotel, where Gran and Scarlett had still been happily chattering away about the investigation they were going to get involved in if and when they managed to drag themselves away from the pleasant surroundings of the hotel's outside dining area and its most delicious offerings of caffeinated beverages and cake. So she had told Gran all about Jane Collins and how happy she and Robert had been together, at least for a little while. As a consequence Gran had taken out her phone and had googled Jane Collins, and before long she had hit upon the right person, or at least she thought she had. "There are three Jane Collinses in Hampton Cove," she said unhappily. "But I'm pretty sure it's this one. What do you think, honey?" She held up her phone so her friend could chime in.

"Oh, I'm sure you're right," said Scarlett easily. "She certainly seems to fit the part."

"The age, Scarlett," Gran insisted. "She needs to fit the right age."

"Well..." Scarlett squinted at the screen. "God, don't tell me I'm going to need reading glasses," she lamented. Finally, she gave up. "You decide," she said. "You're the head of the watch, so you're in charge. And besides, it's your investigation."

"I say this is she," Gran decided. "So let's go and pay her a visit, shall we?" She got up, then sank back down again. "Only... we don't know where she lives."

"Easy peasy. Just call your granddaughter and have her find out."

"I don't want to call Odelia just yet," said Gran. "First I want to make sure we hit the bull's-eye with this one."

"So how do you propose we find out where this Jane Collins person lives?"

"Like you said: easy peasy. We simply call in at the police station."

"But I thought you just said—"

"Just trust me. I know what I'm doing, all right?"

"Uh-oh," said Brutus, and he was right. Every time Gran used those words, things were about to get a little rocky.

Moments later, Gran was in communication with

Dolores, the police station dispatcher. "Yes, this is Mrs. Slater," said Gran in a high-pitched voice. "Marina Slater. I'm a good friend of Jane Collins, and I'm standing right outside her door right now, and I see a bee. So can you send the fire department? I'm sure she's got a nest, and you know how dangerous those nests can be, especially to kids. So send a fire truck and get rid of that nest of dangerous wasps, will you?" She winked at Scarlett, who had listened in through the magic of speakerphone.

"Vesta, I know this is you," said Dolores. "So what's all this about a nest of bees or wasps, and why does your voice sound so weird? Have you been stung yourself, is that it?"

"Oh, but I'm not... Vesta, you said? I'm Marina Slater, a good friend of—"

"Vesta, I can see your number. It says right here on my display that it's you, so stop messing around, will you?"

"Oh, all right," said Gran with an eye roll. "All this technology is killing creativity. So where does she live, this Jane Collins? I need to talk to her."

"Why? What's going on?"

"Nothing important."

"You know I can't just give out people's personal information, right?"

"And why not? Like I said, it's important."

"You just said it's not important!"

"Well, it is and it ain't. It's important to me, but not to you."

"Oh, for crying out loud. I'm putting you through."

"Wait!"

But the deed was done, and Uncle Alec's voice boomed through the phone's speaker. "Now what?" the big man asked.

"I need Jane Collins's address for personal reasons," said

Gran. "And don't tell me you can't give it to me because of privacy. Nobody cares about privacy."

"This wouldn't be connected to the Robert Ross case, would it?"

"Absolutely not. This is neighborhood watch business. Why?"

"Because Chase and Odelia are on their way over there right now."

"No!"

"Yes."

"Give me that address, Alec. They're not going to beat me to it. Not this time!"

"Only if you promise me to behave."

"I always behave!"

"Promise me, Ma."

"Okay, fine. I promise."

"So I won't get any more complaints?"

"What complaints? Who complained?"

"Caroline and Kirk Poots."

"What did they have to complain about?"

"They said you tried to arrest them."

"Nonsense."

"You're not a cop, Ma."

"I know that."

"So don't go around threatening to arrest people."

"Of course not! Who do you think I am? Dirty Harry?"

Uncle Alec grumbled something under his breath, then supplied them with the address for Jane and Bert Collins. The moment Gran hung up, she rubbed her hands with glee. "We're back in business, people! Let's go!"

And so they were off, Gran in an effort to beat her granddaughter and Chase to solve this case, and Brutus and Harriet in a bid to beat Max and Dooley.

The game was afoot!

CHAPTER 21

When we finally arrived at the house where Jane Collins lived, we discovered that we weren't the only ones with a distinct interest in talking to Robert Ross's former girlfriend. The moment Chase pulled the car to a stop, a familiar little red Peugeot also pulled up, and Gran, Scarlett, Harriet, and Brutus spilled out, immediately breaking into a run and heading for the house.

"Now will you look at that," said Chase, sounding amused. "If it ain't the neighborhood watch squad."

"What are they doing here?" asked Odelia, not all that amused.

"Probably the same thing we are: wanting to have a word with Mrs. Collins."

"We better head them off before they try to arrest the poor woman," said Odelia. And so we all hurried out of the car and joined Gran and the others on the front porch of the house. Gran had already pressed her finger to the doorbell, so it looked as if Mrs. Collins would be interviewed by a small committee instead of the customary detective and his loyal sidekick.

"You better let us handle this, Gran," said Odelia.

"And you better let us handle this, Odelia," Gran shot back. "This is our case and we got here first, so we've got dibs on Jane Collins."

"You can't have dibs in a murder inquiry!" said Odelia.

"Of course you can. You can have dibs on anything anytime, and right now, we have first dibs on Jane Collins."

The door opened before Odelia could retort, and from the look on her face, I could tell it would have been a doozy. But when Mrs. Collins suddenly materialized in front of us— or at least I assumed that this was she—the hostilities were momentarily put on hold, and all those present plastered an engaging smile on their faces. Except Chase, who held up his badge instead.

"Chase Kingsley," he announced. "Hampton Cove Police. Jane Collins?"

"That's right," said the woman. She was about Marge's age and was a slender woman with straw-blond hair and a kind face. "What is this about?"

"Can we come in for a moment, Mrs. Collins?"

"I guess so," she said and stepped aside to let the small contingent into her cozy little home. The moment we had all made ourselves comfortable in the living room, she reiterated her earlier question. "What is this all about?"

"I'm sorry to have to inform you, Mrs. Collins," said Chase, taking the lead, "that a former friend of yours has died."

"Yes, I know. Robert Ross? It's been all over the news."

Chase directed a glance at his wife, who blushed slightly, since it was she who had written the article that had informed Mrs. Collins of the death of her former sweetheart. "We've been talking to people who knew Mr. Ross," the reporter explained. "And we've been told that you and Mr. Ross used to be—"

"An item?" asked Mrs. Collins. "That was a long time ago, Miss…"

"Mrs. Kingsley. Odelia Kingsley. And this is my grand-mother Vesta Muffin and her friend Scarlett Canyon. Both members of the neighborhood watch."

If Jane wondered why two members of the watch were present at a police interview, she didn't pose the question. But then stranger things have probably happened, like, for instance, the presence of four cats sitting in on the same interview.

"Look, this was all a very long time ago. Robert and I used to date for a while, but then we split up and I haven't seen the man since."

"Could I ask why you split up?" asked Chase.

"Oh, God. Talk about dredging up the past. It was just one of those things, you know. One of those relationships that simply ran its course. Once we graduated, Robert and I went our separate ways. I went off to study fashion design at the New York School of Design, and Robert started his first year of journalism at NYU. We were supposed to keep seeing each other, but you know how it goes. Once high school is over, everything changes. You meet new people, and high school suddenly feels like a different world. I seem to remember we tried to keep our relationship, if that's what you can call it, going for a while, but eventually things fizzled out. I don't think I've seen him in over twenty years."

"Until this morning," said Gran, giving Jane a close look. The old lady was perched on the edge of the couch and looked ready to spring.

"What do you mean?" asked Jane. "I didn't see Robert this morning."

"Robert was meeting someone this morning," Odelia explained. "He'd asked the crew of the yacht he was traveling on to leave the vessel. So we've been looking for this mystery person, who quite possibly was the last person to see Robert alive."

"Well, it wasn't me," said Jane decidedly. "Like I said, I hadn't seen Robert in over twenty years. I didn't even know he was back in town."

"So he didn't get in touch with you?" asked Chase.

"No, he didn't. And even if he had, I'm not sure I would have gone to meet him. It's been such a long time ago. Like a different life, you know."

"But this Robert wasn't the same Robert you used to know," said Odelia. "Robert Ross had become a famous actor. Weren't you curious to meet him?"

Jane smiled. "Okay, I confess that I've always wondered if he would remember me. For him to become such a major star was beyond the realm of what either of us thought possible at the time. And so as he rose to the top, I often wondered how it would be like to meet again. But then I figured our worlds were so different we wouldn't have anything to talk about."

"Did you become a fashion designer?" asked Scarlett, who's very much into fashion herself, only not as a creator, per se, but more as an avid consumer.

"I did, yes. Only not at the level that I was hoping for at the time. I design sewing patterns that I post on Etsy. People then buy them and make the clothes. It's rewarding work, though maybe not as important as some of the real designers out there designing actual clothes."

"Oh, but you are designing actual clothes," Odelia assured her.

"Thanks. That's very kind of you to say, Mrs. Kingsley. And I do love the work I do, and I get a lot of feedback from happy customers. They even post pictures of the dresses that they created based on my designs, which is very gratifying for me. Though nowadays I'm mostly proud of my family, which I guess is also something I created."

"You and your husband have kids?" asked Chase.

"Four," said Jane with a smile and pointed to a framed picture on the wall behind us. It depicted Jane herself with a round-faced man and four girls. "It's an old picture, taken when the girls were in primary school. They're all grown up now, with only the two youngest ones still living at home. The others have flown the nest, though lucky for us they decided not to move too far away from home. They both live on the same block, as a matter of fact."

"It's probably tough if they move out of state," said Odelia.

"Or out of the country—or to a different continent. My sister's kids both live in Europe, and of course, you want your kids to spread their wings and go where life takes them. But secretly, I'm happy they decided to stay close by."

"Okay," said Chase, all this talk about happy families making him antsy since he had a murder to solve, "so about Robert. He never got in touch with you over the years? Friended you on Facebook? Nothing?"

"Nothing," Jane confirmed. "Not a phone call, not a letter, nothing. And that's fine. I never expected him to. We were only together for a year or so before we split up. And before you ask, there was never a dramatic moment where nasty things were said and doors were slammed. Like I said, our lives took us in different directions and things simply ended."

"So no drama?"

"No drama," said Jane with a smile. "So are you any closer to figuring out who killed him?"

"We're following several promising lines of inquiry," said Chase, giving her the routine answer he always gave when he had no clue what was going on.

"I'm also following some very interesting and promising

lines of inquiry," Gran announced. "Very surprising and very interesting."

"Well, I hope you figure it out," said Jane. "Even though I hadn't seen Robert in a long time, I still held him in my heart, you know."

And since there didn't seem to be anything more to add, we took our leave. Before we left the house, I studied another portrait of the Collins family, this time taken at a later date, where the girls were already a lot bigger than in the big portrait in the living room. They looked like a happy family, I thought, so it was probably a good thing that Robert Ross hadn't been in touch after things had ended between himself and Jane. His particular lifestyle was absolutely not compatible with that of his ex-girlfriend. She may not have become a famous celebrity like himself, but her accomplishments were certainly no less impressive. Quite the contrary, in fact. Whereas Robert had indulged in his hedonistic pleasures, Jane had raised a family, which was no mean feat.

As we stood in the hallway admiring the portrait of the Collins family, Scarlett asked about the presence of any pets in the home.

"No pets, I'm afraid," said Jane. "I'm allergic to both cats and dogs."

"Oh, I'm so sorry," said Odelia. "If I'd known, I wouldn't have brought my cats along."

"It's fine," said Jane. "If it's only for fifteen minutes, I'll be all right. And besides, we have HEPA air purifiers in every room, and if I feel an attack coming on, I have antihistamines and a nasal spray I can use. My sister has cats, you see, so I've become accustomed to taking my precautions. When the girls were little and they used to go over to their aunt's house to play with their cousins, I often took the brunt of it when they got back. But now it's fine."

We said our goodbyes and for a moment stood on the

porch to get our bearings. Unfortunately, we hadn't learned a lot, and I could tell that Gran especially looked very disappointed, and so did Harriet. Clearly, they had harbored high hopes that Jane Collins was the mystery guest Robert Ross had rolled out the red carpet for that morning and possibly was the man's killer.

But from what Jane had told us, this wasn't the case, and I was inclined to believe her. Even though it was possible that Robert had carried a torch for her all these years, or vice versa, it was also highly unlikely. As she had said, they had both gone their separate ways without a lot of drama involved.

The question remained: why had he turned down all invitations from the Chamber of Commerce for fifteen years and suddenly decided to accept? Though there was probably a simple explanation: age. When men got older, they started thinking about their legacy. So maybe Robert had reached the age where he wondered how he would be remembered. And a nice award and some media attention from his home town would probably hit the spot.

And we had just crawled back into Chase's squad car when another car pulled up in front of the house and a man hurried out. I recognized him from the many family pictures in the Collins house: this was Jane's husband, Bert.

He glanced over, then approached us. "Detective Kingsley?" he asked. "My name is Bert Collins. Jane's husband. Have you talked to my wife yet?"

"We have," Chase confirmed. "We were just leaving."

"I'm sorry. I was held up at work. Can I..." He seemed irresolute for a moment, then suddenly got into the car and closed the door. "Could we go for a drive? There's something I need to tell you."

Chase glanced over at his wife, who shrugged, and so the cop put the car in gear, and moments later, we were cruising the neighborhood, Dooley and I in the company of Bert Collins.

"Can you tell us what this is all about?" asked Chase, clearly not all that happy with all this cloak-and-dagger stuff.

"It's my wife," said Bert finally. "I have to ask you not to contact her again." And when only a stunned silence met these words, he added, "She's not well."

CHAPTER 22

*C*hase drove slow circles around the block while Bert Collins told his tale.

"She's been suffering from severe depression for years," he explained. "It all began after Alice was born, our youngest, and hasn't really improved much since. She's been taking medication and has been seeing a shrink, and that has taken the edge off the dark moods she oftentimes falls prey to, and mostly we think we've got it under control now, but from time to time she will sink back down into the darkness, and it can take her days to emerge again. Right now, she's doing pretty well, so I would very much like to keep it that way. And being exposed to all this murder business won't do her a lot of good."

"We had to ask her a couple of questions," said Odelia. "Seeing as she used to know the victim."

"Twenty-five years ago!" said Bert. "I really don't see how that's relevant. She hadn't met the guy in years, and even when they were in school together, they were only an item for a few short months. What are a couple of months over a lifetime? Nothing. So I really don't see why you have to confront her with all of that."

"We asked her all the questions we needed to ask, and your wife answered them all," said Odelia reassuringly. "So as things now stand, we don't have to talk to her again."

"Unless new information surfaces," Chase pointed out.

"It won't," Bert said emphatically. "She never had anything to do with the guy, and so I would very much like your confirmation that this is the end of it."

"We can't give you that reassurance, Mr. Collins," said Odelia. "But like I said, most likely we won't have to talk to your wife again."

It seemed to be good enough for the guy, for he grunted with satisfaction. "It's been hell on our family, as you can imagine. And with two of our daughters still living at home, it hasn't been easy. Not for them, not for me, but most of all not for Jane."

"What do you think brought this all on?"

"According to the doctors, it all started with post-partum depression, which lingered and never completely went away. She was fine with our previous girls and never suffered any post-partum depressions then. But with Alice…" He sagged a little, looking tired and wan, I now determined. "I don't know. I'm not a mental health expert, obviously. As far as I can understand, it has something to do with a chemical imbalance in the brain, brought on by the hormonal impact of the pregnancy. But why it wouldn't simply go away again beats me."

"I'm very sorry, Mr. Collins," said Odelia, and I could tell that her concern was heartfelt and sincere. Having gone through a pregnancy herself, perhaps she had experienced some of what Mrs. Collins was feeling.

"It's fine," said Bert, putting on a brave face. "We're fine. As long as she doesn't get bad news or something that upsets her, mostly my wife is okay. We all try to shield her from most of it. We don't subscribe to any newspapers and don't leave them lying around the house. We don't watch a lot of television, for the least little thing might trigger her and cause her to fall off a cliff. Mostly we try to ensure that the atmosphere around the house is uplifting and positive."

"And her sewing designs must also be a great blessing for her," said Odelia.

Bert nodded. "She loves to do those. And the response has been overwhelmingly positive. Every time she posts a new design, it's heart-warming to see how many people leave positive comments and absolutely adore her work."

"I'll check it out myself tonight," Odelia promised. "And if you like, I could even do an article on it for the *Gazette*."

He gave her a grateful smile. "That would be great. We don't take the *Gazette*, for the same reason I already told you, but I'll show her the article." Then a look of concern clouded his mostly sunny demeanor. "You wouldn't have to interview her for the article, would you?"

"If you don't want me to, I won't. Though of course, it would be great if I could chat with her about it. Mostly it would be about her designs, nothing else."

"I guess that would be fine," he said thoughtfully. Clearly, his life revolved around making sure that Jane was shielded as much as possible from any adverse influences that could trigger one of her depressive episodes.

We had circled back to the house, and he now got out, thanking us for our understanding and also apologizing for any inconvenience this might have caused to our investigation. Chase assured him that he had all the information from Jane that he needed, and we watched as the man hurried up the drive and disappeared inside.

"Must be tough to live like that," said Chase. "Always

having to walk on eggshells, worried that the least little comment or incident might trigger an episode."

"Must be tough on the kids as well," said Odelia. "Kids mostly don't have a filter and just blab about whatever comes to mind. And now they have to consider that their words might have an adverse effect on their mom."

"So do you think Jane was Robert's mystery guest, Max?" asked Dooley.

"I'm not sure," I confessed. "Though she seemed truthful when she said she hadn't seen her ex-boyfriend in years."

"I think she was telling the truth," Odelia said, adding her two cents to the conversation. "It's only natural that when kids leave school, these old friendships and relationships change, and they go their separate ways. What she described to us in there was a boy-girl relationship that lasted a couple of months and ended in a natural way, with no regrets on either side."

"So you don't think Robert's sudden return to Hampton Cove was motivated by his sudden wish to reunite with his old girlfriend?" asked Chase.

"I doubt it, babe," said Odelia. "Clearly, she hadn't thought of the guy in many years, having built a family of her own, and I think the same thing could probably be said about Robert, who had built an impressive career and had left Hampton Cove and any attachments he may have formed in his rear-view mirror a long time ago."

"I wonder where Flame could be," I now said, deciding to change the topic. "We still have to talk to her, remember?"

"Oh, she's with Robert's brother," said Odelia. "We're going to talk to the man now, and then you and Dooley can chat with Flame. Though I think we pretty much know what was in Robert's safe and who emptied it out."

"Money and drugs," I said. "Presumably handed over to

Sebastian Poe as compensation for the misery they had put the man through."

"Do you think Poe was the carjacker who attacked Chantal last night?" asked Dooley.

"It wouldn't surprise me if it was," I said. "Clearly, the man wasn't in a fit state, judging from what we heard from the crew members." And since Sarah Flunk had put out an APB on Chantal's car, hopefully we would catch up with Mr. Poe at some point in the near future and put the question to him. As things now stood, I felt that he should be our main suspect for Mr. Ross's murder, and I had a feeling that Chase and Odelia felt the same way.

BEFORE LONG, we arrived at the Star Hotel, which is a five-star hotel in the heart of town. Mr. Ross's brother had arrived to make the necessary funeral arrangements for Robert and also to collect his personal belongings from the Aurora and make any final payments to the crew that were necessary.

We found him in the lobby of the hotel, where he got up the moment we walked in. He resembled his brother in the fact that he was tall and handsome with slicked-back dark hair. Only he was of a more intellectual bent, with a pair of fashionable glasses lending him a lawyerly look. If Robert was Superman, this man looked more like Clark Kent.

"Thank you for seeing us on such short notice, Mr. Ross," said Odelia, shaking the man's hand. "And I'm very sorry for your loss."

"Thank you," said the man. "And I'm only happy to assist you in finding my brother's murderer. Are you any closer to identifying the person responsible?"

The humans had all taken a seat on one of the plush couches located in the lobby, while Dooley and I hovered nearby, lending a listening ear and generally hoping to glean more information that could assist us in forming a picture of the deceased. The more you know about the victim, the more likely it is that you can figure out why he was killed, and consequently by whom.

"We're pursuing several promising lines of inquiry," Chase said, once again using the old standby. "So what can you tell us about your brother, Mr. Ross? Did he have any enemies that you know of, grudges people had against him? Threats that were made in the recent past?"

"Before we begin," said Odelia, interrupting the proceedings, "can you tell us where Flame is?"

Mr. Ross—Eric to his friends—gave her a strange look. "She's upstairs in my room. Why?"

"No reason. Just wanted to make sure she was well taken care of."

He smiled. "I'd heard that you love animals, Mrs. Kingsley. And there's absolutely no reason to be concerned about Flame. I'll take very good care of my brother's beloved Papillon. We have several dogs ourselves, Valerie and I, and I'm sure Flame will fit in well with them. Now, as to any threats being made against my brother, as you can imagine there were many over the years. But if you want details, you should probably contact his agent, who will have them all logged, just in case one of them actually materialized. But an actor of his stature always gets threatening emails, messages, and letters. It's all part of being in the public eye to such an extent. But as far as I could tell, Robert was never too concerned about any of that. He said it was part and parcel of being a star, and he didn't pay any notice to any of that stuff."

"So nothing that jumped out at him? Something that he talked to you about?" asked Chase.

"Nothing like that," Eric assured us. "Though like I said, most of the threats he received were blocked at the level of his team. I don't think they even passed them on to him, effectively acting as a filter between my brother and the big bad world outside. I often told him that he lived in a bubble, and he admitted that he did. But he said it was necessary, and that most of the stars at his level lived like that, otherwise they wouldn't be able to function."

"We'll talk to his agent," Chase said, making a note in his notebook. "Is there anything else you can think of that might be relevant? Any concerns your brother voiced recently? Things that kept him up at night? Or changes in his general behavior? Something that jumped out?"

"Not that I can think of," said Eric as he turned pensive for a moment. "He did seem more… reflective lately. Philosophical, even. Talked about our childhood, our mom and dad, how life was when we were boys together."

"Are they still with us, your mom and dad?" asked Odelia.

"Oh, yes, although they both live in Florida now. Once Robert started making some serious money, he bought them a nice place in Palm Beach, and they've lived there ever since, having a ball. They retired and moved out there. They both took up golf, and they've been terrorizing the local community by driving everywhere in their golf carts. But they're happy and healthy, and that's what counts. Though Robert's murder has come as a big shock to them, of course. They adored my brother, as did we all. To see him go from strength to strength and effectively turn into a global star was amazing to watch."

"Did you still see a lot of him?"

"Oh, absolutely. We met up for the holidays, and birthdays. He was also the godfather to my girls, and he adored them. Not having any kids of his own, he doted on them and spoiled them, probably too much, I'd say. He got them ponies for their twelfth birthday, which was a gift that was much appreciated, though maybe a little too much," he said with a grin.

"What is it that you do, Mr. Ross?" asked Chase.

"I'm a lawyer," said the man. "In fact, I was part of my brother's legal team. As you can imagine, being an actor of his stature comes with a lot of legal threats as well as the usual garbage on social media. So that kept us busy enough. And handling contracts, of course."

"Any legal threats that could have a bearing on our case?" asked Chase.

The lawyer thought for a moment. "Well... there is this one actor who claims that he should have gotten the part of James Fox back in the day. He and Robert were both in the running for the role at the time, but eventually Robert won out. And now the guy claims that his audition tape mysteriously disappeared, and that Robert was instrumental in making it so. Nonsense, of course, but still something we need to deal with, as he decided to take matters to court. It's all noise, you know, and very annoying, but it comes with the territory."

"Who is this guy?" asked Chase.

Eric Ross supplied him with the name of the actor and his details, and the detective dutifully jotted it all down. It felt like a long shot, but in cases like these, it's important to be thorough, and that was certainly Chase's intention.

As the conversation continued, Odelia gave us a sign that I interpreted as our cue to go in search of Flame, to conduct our own interview. And even though I had no idea how we would go about finding her or getting access to her if she was locked up in the lawyer's room, we still did as we were told. We hadn't even crossed the lobby to the bank of elevators when Odelia hurried up to join us.

"I told him I had to go to the bathroom," she whispered,

then pressed her finger on the elevator button, and moments later we stepped inside.

"How are you going to get us inside the man's room?" I asked.

Which is when Odelia held up a key card with a triumphant look. "Don't ask me how I did it," she said, "but this should get us in without a problem!"

"How did you do it?" asked Dooley without missing a beat.

"I asked Kevin, Scarlett's great-nephew. He temps here."

"In other words," said Dooley, "it's an inside job."

CHAPTER 23

It wasn't just the fact that Odelia wanted Max and Dooley to have another little chat with Robert's dog, but also that she wanted to take a closer look at Eric Ross's room. Somehow she felt that the man was just a little bit too glib and too much 'sunshine and roses' when it came to describing his relationship with his famous sibling, so she felt it wouldn't be a bad idea to go through his personal belongings, hoping to find something that could be of interest.

She might be a civilian consultant, but first and foremost she was a reporter, and since reporters can't rely on court orders and search warrants to take a closer look at the targets of their investigations, she had decided to search the man's room the old-fashioned way: by breaking and entering quite illegally!

If Chase knew, he probably wouldn't have approved, which is why she had decided not to clue him in. The term 'plausible deniability' sprang to mind, though she was fairly sure that she wouldn't be caught. In and out, as quick as she could, that was the ticket.

So she looked left and right, checked if no one saw her go in, inserted the keycard Kevin had printed into the lock, and stole into the room. For a lawyer, the man wasn't all that neat, she saw. Shirts had been thrown on the bed, towels on the floor, and the TV still stood blaring in a corner of the room, depicting a number of talking heads screaming at each other about some matter of little importance.

"Dooley!" she said. "You watch the door! Max! You talk to Flame!"

And so Dooley positioned himself in front of the door, watching it intently. She had to physically pick him up and put him out in the corridor and tell him that when she said 'Watch the door,' she didn't actually mean that he had to watch the door, but more that he had to watch out for the arrival of Eric Ross and warn them.

Max, meanwhile, had located Flame, who was reposing on the floor in a shaft of sunlight slanting in through the window, and looked up when the trio arrived but didn't bark, which proved once and for all that Papillons are lovely companions but perhaps not all that great watchdogs.

Donning plastic gloves for the occasion, she quickly moved over to the man's laptop, which was on a small table near the television, and as luck would have it, Eric hadn't closed it or hit the screen lock. Sloppy, she thought as she quickly started searching through the man's emails. At first sight, she found nothing out of the ordinary, but when she had scrolled down a couple of days, she suddenly saw a subject line that looked promising. 'How to deal with the fallout from the Sebastian Poe affair,' it read, and when she opened it, her eyes quickly scanning its contents, a smile curved up her face. Now this was something she could work with.

Apparently, Robert had told his brother about what happened to Sebastian Poe and the man's unfortunate demise at his hands and had asked the lawyer to handle the possible fallout of Poe's disappearance. Eric had advised his brother to keep his cool and that when the police came looking for Poe, to deny that he had ever laid eyes on the man.

'Denial is your strongest defense,' he had written to his brother. 'So deny, deny, deny.'

To which Robert had replied, 'You're a real lifesaver, little brother. Thanks a million!'

Apparently, Robert had been concerned about what he'd done to Poe and had decided to prime his legal team in case Poe's body was found floating not far from where the Aurora had been the night of the man's disappearance.

So Eric had known all about what happened to Poe and had decided to ride out the storm and use consistent denial as their strategy.

She scrolled through the emails some more, but nothing else struck her as important or relevant. And as she straightened again, wondering what else she should be looking for, suddenly there was a tap at the window, and she jumped about a foot in the air. As she placed a hand on her beating heart, she saw to her surprise that her grandmother's face had suddenly materialized in the balcony window!

She opened the balcony door and hissed, "Gran, what are you doing here?"

"I climbed over from the next balcony," Gran explained, as if it was the most natural thing in the world. And Odelia could see that Scarlett was just about to do the same thing.

"You shouldn't be here!" she said.

"Nor should you," said Gran matter-of-factly and stepped into the room, intently looking left and right for a sign of whatever she had come there to do.

Scarlett had now joined them, and also Harriet and Brutus, so the neighborhood watch was complete. "Vesta figured that Robert's brother might make a good suspect,"

145

she explained. "So we're going to expose the man and bring him to justice for what he's done."

"But why? Why would Eric kill his own brother?" Odelia asked.

Scarlett shrugged. "Beats me. You'd have to ask Vesta. She's the brains in this outfit of ours."

Odelia turned her eyes heavenward. "If Gran is the brains of the watch, God help us all."

"Hey, I heard that!" Gran called out. "And I'll have you know that I've got good reason to believe that the brother did it."

"What reason would that be?" asked Odelia, folding her arms across her chest and tapping her foot impatiently. If Eric suddenly decided to go up to his room to pick up his laptop, they were all done for and liable to be arrested for trespassing.

"Look, it's simple," said Gran. "When someone is murdered, it's always the spouse that did it, right?"

"Or the butler," Scarlett pointed out helpfully.

"Or the butler," Gran allowed. "But in this case, Robert didn't have a wife, so we now move to the next closest relative, which is his siblings, and since he only had the one brother, he must have killed him."

"But why? Why would Eric kill his own brother?" Odelia asked again.

"Sibling rivalry," said Gran. "He was jealous of Robert's success and finally couldn't stand it anymore, so he whacked him." She shook her head. "It's always the quiet ones you have to watch out for. Now, where is that cyanide?"

She was rifling through the man's suitcase in search of this elusive vial of cyanide.

"You won't find it," Odelia told her grandmother. "No killer worth his salt would keep such incriminating evidence lying around."

"Got it!" Gran suddenly yelled and held up a small bottle with a clear liquid inside. "See? I told you the guy was guilty. And now we've got the evidence to prove it!"

"Let me see that," said Odelia and took the bottle from her gran, who had been handling it without gloves, of course, adding her own fingerprints to whatever prints were already on the vial. When she studied it a little closer, she saw it was insulin.

"And look here!" said Gran, holding up a syringe. "This is the murder weapon right here! Busted, buddy, and all hail to the watch!"

"All hail to the watch," Scarlett murmured.

"This is insulin!" said Odelia, who couldn't believe her quiet and discreet operation had been turned into some kind of vaudeville all of a sudden. "Eric is probably a diabetic. And that's the syringe he uses to inject himself with."

"Insulin?" asked Gran. "Are you sure?"

"Absolutely. Now I suggest you both leave the same way you came, but first we put everything back the way we found it, before Eric finds out we've been searching his room without a search warrant."

"I could have sworn..." Gran murmured as she checked the vial again. She frowned. "Are you sure he killed him with cyanide? You can kill a person with an overdose of insulin, you know."

"Yes, I'm sure," she said. "Now please get out, Gran, before we're all caught!"

"We won't get caught," said Scarlett. "I asked Kevin to keep a lookout downstairs. The moment Eric heads to the elevator, he'll send me a message." She held up her phone. "The watch is always prepared!"

"Okay, so maybe you're right," said Gran finally, "and this isn't cyanide. So that means we need to dig deeper." And to show them she wasn't kidding, she began digging through the man's personal belongings with even more vigor than before! Odelia watched it with a rising sense of panic. If Eric found his room ransacked, he'd call the police—in other words, Chase. And he would have to investigate, possibly discovering that his own wife had been there, as well as Gran and Scarlett!

"Will you please leave that alone!" she said. "And get out of here!"

"We're not leaving until we've hit on conclusive evidence that this man killed his own brother," Gran said adamantly. "Now what else is there?" She had swiveled around and now spotted the laptop. "A-hah!" she cried and made a beeline for the device. Quickly scanning its contents, she said, "The guy is clearly a pervert. He's got funny pictures on here!"

"What funny pictures?" asked Odelia, against her better judgment joining her grandmother. There were pictures of two young girls playing on a beach, dressed in bathing suits. "Probably his daughters," she said.

"A likely story! As I see it, Robert found out that his brother was into funny business, and so he threatened to go to the cops, which is when Eric decided to get rid of his brother."

"They're his daughters!"

"I'm confiscating this here laptop as evidence," Gran said. "Bag it, Scarlett."

"Huh?" said Scarlett.

"Bag and tag, honey!"

"What?"

Just then, the door of the room opened, and Eric burst in. When he saw Odelia and her grandmother standing over his laptop, he yelled, "What the hell do you think you're doing?"

But Gran had her response ready. Stepping to the fore, she said, "Eric Ross, I'm arresting you on suspicion of the possession of lewd images of a, um, well, of a lewd nature."

Lucky for them, Chase now walked in, so Odelia decided to show him the emails Eric had exchanged with his brother about the Poe affair. And since Eric was on the verge of assailing Gran, he decided to ask the man to join him at the police station for further questioning.

"You shouldn't have been in my room," the lawyer protested. "This is a sting operation, and my lawyers will have a field day with you bunch of clowns. By the time we're through with you, you'll all be out of a job—that is a promise!"

Chase led the man away, but Odelia knew that maybe the lawyer had a point. Anything seized during an illegal search of his room was most likely inaccessible in court.

"Well done, honey," said Gran, blithely ignorant of the havoc she had caused and the potential legal nightmare they were facing when Eric Ross unleashed his team of barracuda lawyers on them. "We've arrested a predator and a murderer, so we should celebrate!"

"Why didn't Kevin warn us the guy was coming?" asked Scarlett and took out her phone to call her great-nephew. "He was probably flirting with a guest again. Oh, that boy…"

"And why didn't Dooley warn us?" asked Odelia. But when she went in search of her cat, she saw that Dooley was still positioned in front of the door.

"Mr. Ross arrived, Odelia," he said happily. "But then he left again."

She closed her eyes. Maybe next time her instructions should be even more specific. Or maybe she should put Max in charge of watching the door, and Dooley in charge of interviewing the damn dog!

CHAPTER 24

*W*hile Odelia and Gran were conducting their investigation, I had a quiet chat with Flame. The dog didn't seem surprised to see us. "I figured you'd want to have another talk with me, Max," she said. "I've been thinking about what happened the last couple of days before Robert died and have been trying to puzzle together what I think must have gone down."

"And what do you think happened?" I asked.

The doggie had straightened a little and gave me a look of concern. "I'm starting to think that maybe there was some kind of conspiracy to get rid of my human, Max. I mean, why did all the crew members leave the ship at the exact time the killer arrived? And why did they decide to remove me from the scene? The only thing I can think of is that the crew must have conspired with the killer. Or maybe one of them was the actual killer."

"It's certainly possible," I agreed. "Though why do you think they would have wanted to murder their employer?" I had my own suspicions, but I wanted to hear it from Flame.

"Well, there's Suzanne Palmer, of course. I guess by now

she must have told you all about what happened between her and Robert?"

"She did," I said. "Robert harassed her to such an extent she saw no other recourse than to hit him over the head with his Golden Globe, resulting in ten stitches to his forehead and a nasty scar."

"He was actually secretly proud of his scar, you know," said Flame with a sad smile. "I caught him posing in front of the mirror and studying that scar, then quoting lines from gangster movies. I think he thought he looked pretty tough now with that scar and might go from playing the hero to being the bad guy for a change."

"So do you think Suzanne decided to get rid of Robert once and for all?" I asked.

"I'm not sure. There's something I need to tell you, Max. It had slipped my mind, but a couple of days before Robert died, he got a call from his agent, who told him that the production company and the studio had decided to terminate his contract for the James Fox movies. Apparently, his behavior was cause for concern, and they had decided they were going with a different actor going forward."

"So Robert was being fired?"

"That's right. According to the agent, Robert had caused them so much embarrassment with his outrageous behavior that they saw grounds for his dismissal. Robert said he was going to fight them on it, but the agent said there wasn't a lot he could do since it clearly stated in his contract that he had a morality clause to prevent exactly this type of behavior that might cause embarrassment to the studio or the James Fox brand. And his behavior, as ascertained by several anonymous witness accounts, was clearly in violation of this clause."

"So one of the crew members had talked to the production company or the studio, and they had decided to sever all ties with Robert based on his or her testimony."

Flame nodded. "Robert was very upset about it, as you can imagine, since his entire career revolved around being the actor that played James Fox. And he swore to get back at the production company, the crew member who had blabbed, and even his agent. He said he had collected a lot of dirt on them over the years and he wouldn't hesitate to give it all to the first reporter who asked."

"What dirt would this be?" I asked.

"I think he was bluffing," said Flame. "And the agent seemed to feel the same way, for he said Robert should cool his jets and simply ride out the storm. And maybe also clean up his act and apologize to the crew and to the producers. Then maybe he still stood a chance to reverse the decision. He even got him hired for a side project about Napoleon Bonaparte's relationship with Josephine. But if he started hurling threats around, his career just might be over. But then Robert wasn't thinking straight. All those pills he had been taking, and the copious amounts of alcohol he consumed, and the rest of it, had affected his mental capacities and also his judgment." She smiled. "But at least he still cared about me. That never changed."

"And you cared about him."

"Of course I did. Deep down he was a good man. He had simply lost his way. But with a little bit of encouragement, I'm convinced he would have found it again. If only he had met the right woman. She could have straightened him out. And I think he knew this. Which is probably why he decided to return to Hampton Cove. To somehow rediscover the old Robert. The person he used to be before his success had gone to his head and made him go a little crazy."

"Who was the crew member who blabbed about Robert to his producers, you think?"

"Oh, he knew exactly who it was. Marcus O'Reilly."

"Marcus! But I thought he was Robert's biggest supporter."

"He was. Until he discovered that Robert had been stringing him along. He had promised Marcus a part in his next James Fox movie, so Marcus went ahead and contacted Robert's agent, figuring the thing was in the bag. But when the agent called Robert and asked him about it, he said he'd just said that to keep Marcus happy and that he never intended to give him any part in any movie. So when the agent turned Marcus down, there was a big screaming row between Robert and Marcus, who said Robert had betrayed him. Robert told him to go to hell, and Marcus said he would, and he would take Robert along with him."

"Wow," I said. "Marcus did not tell us that."

"I'll bet he didn't. Though to be honest, I don't think the guy has it in him to murder people, Max. And besides, poisoning a person is a woman's crime, right?"

"I very much doubt that, Flame," I said. "I think you'll find that anyone can murder anyone with any type of weapon, whether it be knives, guns, or poison."

"I guess you're the expert."

"There's one more thing I need to ask you. The safe. What was in it, do you know?"

"Well, he kept his stash in there," said Flame. "Money and drugs."

"But when we arrived on the boat this morning, it was empty."

"That's because he handed everything in that safe to Sebastian Poe. Didn't I tell you?"

"No, you didn't."

"Well, as I already told you, Poe came to visit him last night. And I think it's safe to say Robert freaked out big time when he saw the man, since he had supposed that he was dead. We all did. But there he was, alive and well. Okay, maybe not so well, since he looked terrible. But definitely alive. And so after ascertaining that Poe was indeed the man he said he was, Robert sort of collapsed into a heap and started blubbering and wailing and apologizing to his old friend. He said the whole thing had been an accident and he had never wanted to hurt him. But Poe had said some nasty things, and so he had thrown that bottle at him, not knowing how awful the consequences would be. They talked for hours, and finally, Poe said he forgave him, and that as far as he was concerned, they could be friends again. It was a pretty bizarre scene, to be honest, and I wasn't sure what to think of it. Poe behaved really strangely, as if he wasn't all there. He said he'd been living on some island, and gotten himself in some kind of trouble and now he needed money. Lots of it."

"And so Robert gave him the contents of his safe?"

"Yes. Every last cent and also all of his pills and the drugs —all of it. Poe said he'd sell everything and use the money as a kind of dowry. He said he'd gotten the daughter of the tribe leader pregnant, and if he didn't marry her and provide for her, they might kill him."

"Sounds like he really got himself in a pickle."

"I'm not sure I bought all of that, to be honest. Like I said, Poe was behaving erratically. But Robert believed every word and said he was so happy that his friend was still alive."

"And then Poe left with the money."

Flame nodded. "I know you think Poe killed Robert, but I'm not so sure he did. Why kill the goose that lays the golden eggs? Robert was a lot more useful to him alive than dead. He could always come back to demand more money, and Robert would have given it to him, no questions asked."

"Yeah, I guess you're right," I said. "Unless he was so upset about what happened that he decided to get even. Like you said, he wasn't thinking straight, and in his erratic state of mind, he might have decided to kill his friend."

"It's possible," said Flame. "But I still think it was Suzanne Palmer."

I nodded and thanked the doggie for her candid testimony. It couldn't be easy to spill the beans on her human like that. I know that if I ever had to testify against Odelia, I wouldn't like to tell all about her private stuff to a complete stranger. "So are you going to be all right now, Flame?" I asked.

"Oh, absolutely," said Flame. "Eric is a nice guy. I've met him many times, and he loves dogs. So I'll become part of his family now, and I'm sure I'll be fine." She sighed. "Though of course, I'll always miss Robert."

"I know you will," I said.

We looked up when the scene around us seemed to turn even more animated than it had been before. And when all of a sudden Eric Ross was led away, I thought I detected a note of concern in Flame's voice when she said, "And the hits, they just keep on coming!"

CHAPTER 25

*O*delia felt a little nervous when she accompanied her grandmother and Scarlett to the police station. Her uncle had summoned them after Eric Ross's arrest, and that could only mean one thing: that the man's lawyers had decided to question the validity of the search of his hotel room, claiming they had violated his right to privacy, and that any evidence found was inadmissible and should be thrown out by the judge in case their client was arraigned.

"You shouldn't have gone in there," Gran said as they drove to the station.

"I shouldn't have gone in there! How about *you* shouldn't have gone in!"

"I had every right as a member of the watch," Gran claimed. The old lady was in the passenger seat while Odelia drove her old truck to the police station, with Scarlett in the back with the cats. "I looked it up, and it's called the plain view doctrine. When you see evidence of a crime through the window, you're allowed to seize said evidence without a warrant."

"Gran, you're not a cop! You can't just go barging into people's hotel rooms and search through their stuff."

"The same goes for you," Gran pointed out. "So I guess we're both in the wrong, and I'm sure your uncle will give us hell." She sighed. "Why I raised that boy to be a cop, I'll never know. Now if he had followed my advice and run for mayor instead, this would never have happened."

"How do you figure that!" said Odelia.

"Well, as we all know, the mayor is the boss of the police. So whatever he says goes. So if Alec had been mayor, he would have made short shrift of all this privacy nonsense. Besides, perverts don't have a right to privacy. So I'm glad we caught this monster, and I hope they'll lock him up for the rest of his life."

"Fat chance," said Odelia. With the unlawful search, the judge would have no other recourse than to let the man go. Or at least that's how she read the situation. She wasn't a lawyer, of course, so she could be wrong. The four cats had been conspicuously quiet, and she now glanced at them through the rear-view mirror. "So how did it go with Flame, Max?"

"She thinks that Suzanne Palmer did it," Max announced. "Figuring hitting him with that Golden Globe didn't get the message across and deciding to finish the job. Though I doubt it. Suzanne doesn't seem the type to go around poisoning her employers, even if they are jerks. Oh, and Robert had recently been fired from his job as James Fox. The production company had received several complaints from a crew member—all anonymous, though Ross knew it was Marcus O'Reilly. To spare themselves any possible embarrassment in the future, the producers decided to cut the actor loose and hire a new guy to play James Fox. Though it could be a woman, of course. Though they'd probably have to change the name."

157

"We'll have to talk to Robert's agent," said Odelia, making a mental note. "Anything else?"

"Yeah, that Poe was the one who received the contents of his friend's safe last night. He said he was going to marry the daughter of the chief of the tribe he'd been staying with, and he needed to pay dowry to the girl's family after he got her pregnant."

"Now that is a system I like," said Gran. "If only it existed here, then Chase would have had to pay me so he could marry you."

"I think you'll find that if that were the case, Chase would have had to pay Dad," Odelia pointed out.

"Same difference." She turned to her friend. "Did you get all that, honey?"

"What did I get?" asked Scarlett.

"What Max just told us?"

"You know that I don't understand your cats, Vesta," said Scarlett. "So I'm afraid you'll have to translate."

And so Gran did and told her friend all about what Flame had told Max. By the time the story was done, and they had discussed the ins and outs of the case, she parked her car in the police station parking lot, and they all got out. Normally she wasn't nervous about being summoned to her uncle's office, but now she was. Somehow she had a feeling he wouldn't be pleased with them.

They passed the reception desk where Dolores Peltz was busy talking on the phone. As they walked by, the woman made a slicing gesture with her hand across her throat, and that told Odelia all she needed to know about their upcoming interview with her uncle.

"Don't you worry about a thing, honey," said Gran, who must have sensed how nervous she was. "If things turn ugly, I'll fix him."

"Fix him? What do you mean, fix him?"

"I'll simply tell him I withdraw my consent to that marriage of his to Charlene."

"Uncle Alec is a grown man, Gran. He doesn't need your consent."

"Times sure are a-changing," Gran grumbled.

They had arrived at her uncle's office, and she would have politely knocked and awaited his response, but her grand-mother had different ideas and barged into the office without knocking. "What's all this about you wanting to see us?!" she demanded heatedly, planting her fists on her hips and positioning herself in front of her son's desk. "Don't you think we've got better things to do than to spend our precious time in this skanky office of yours?"

"Sit down," said Uncle Alec.

"I won't be spoken to like that!"

"Sit. Down!"

And Gran sat down, and so did Scarlett and Odelia. Even the cats sat down on the floor and awaited further develop-ments with bated breath.

Uncle Alec raked their visages with a kindling eye, then spoke. "You have all broken the law by breaking into the hotel room of a well-respected member of the public."

"He's a known child molester!" Gran cried.

"He is not. The whole thing rests on a misunderstanding, and if you had simply—"

"What misunderstanding? We all saw the pictures!"

"Pictures of Eric Ross's daughters on the beach. Dressed in bathing suits. There's nothing illegal about it."

"But—"

"Nothing illegal whatsoever! The only thing that was illegal was the three of you breaking into the man's hotel room, going through his personal belongings, even going so far as to read his emails! Do you realize the trouble you're in?"

"But—"

"The man is a prominent lawyer! With a very litigious law firm. They will have a field day with this whole business. Not to mention the fact that we still haven't been able to catch whoever killed the man's brother, making us look like a bunch of incompetent bumbling bungling idiots!"

"The Keystone Kops," Dooley said happily, a statement Odelia decided not to translate.

"I'm pretty sure there were more pictures," Gran said stubbornly. "Only the guy came busting in so we couldn't take a better look."

"I can assure you that his computer was thoroughly searched, and no incriminating pictures were found," said Uncle Alec. "So not only have you managed to antagonize the victim's brother, but you have put this department in the crosshairs of a bunch of ravenous lawyers. These people are like piranhas, they can smell blood in the water and then they move in for the kill."

"The Keystone Kops versus the Piranha Lawyers," said Dooley happily. "That's a movie I want to see, Max."

"Not me," Max murmured.

"Look, I can understand you acted from the noblest of intentions," said Odelia's uncle, folding his hands on his desk blotter, "but I still have to ask: what the hell were you thinking!"

"I was thinking that we had ourselves a killer to catch," said Gran. "And to my mind, the ends justify the means, Alec. That man!" she cried, pointing in the general direction of the door. "Killed his own brother! And you're letting him get away with it!"

"What makes you think he killed Robert? What evidence do you have?"

"It stands to reason, doesn't it?" She held up her index finger. "Motive! Robert was a major movie star. So obviously, the guy was jealous of his brother. Opportunity! It's not difficult to sneak aboard a ship. Either you swim or you row a boat out. Means! He had access to the cyanide."

"How? The guy is a lawyer, Ma, not a pharmacist."

"Oh, you can buy that stuff online nowadays. Heck, I could order a vial of cyanide on the dark web if I wanted to."

A slight smile momentarily flickered up Uncle Alec's lips. "What do you know about the dark web, Ma?"

"Plenty! I know it's the web, and I know it's dark."

"Oh, God," said the Chief and rubbed his face with his hands. "What am I going to do with you?"

"Are we in trouble, Uncle Alec?" asked Odelia. "I mean, in legal trouble?"

"Oh, he'll sue, that's for sure," said her uncle. "He'll sue the department, he'll sue the town, he'll sue you three. Heck, he'll probably sue us all!" He looked up. "Unless..."

Hope surged in Odelia's bosom. "Unless what?"

"Unless you catch his brother's killer. I can't imagine he'd sue the officers who were instrumental in capturing his brother's murderer. Catch me a killer, and this will all go away. He'll drop his complaint, drop the lawsuit, and probably be happy as a clam that we've managed to bring Robert's killer to justice. Because make no mistake—the guy adored his big brother."

"A likely story," said Gran.

"Well, he did. Robert was like a hero to him. The guy who made it big."

"If that guy was a hero, I'm Peppa Pig," Gran grunted unhappily.

"And if we don't catch Robert's killer?" asked Scarlett now. Unlike Gran, she didn't look happy with the way things had gone. She even looked scared.

The Chief's face sagged. "Then God help us all."

CHAPTER 26

"Why does Gran want to be Peppa the Pig, Max?" asked Dooley. "And who is Peppa the Pig?"

"Peppa Pig is a cartoon for kids," I explained. "About a pig named Peppa."

"I don't think Gran wants to be Peppa Pig," said Brutus. "And besides, she's a human, not a pig."

"She could change her name to Peppa," Harriet pointed out.

"Trademarked," Brutus grunted. "So she couldn't even if she wanted to."

"I think you can call yourself Peppa if you wanted to," I said. "The same way you could call yourself Mickey or Donald or Goofy or any cartoon character's name."

"I want to be called Garfield from now on," said Dooley. "I like Garfield. Though I don't understand why he likes lasagna so much."

"It's meat and cheese," said Brutus. "What's not to like?"

"If I could pick a name for myself, it would be Céline," said Harriet.

"Céline is not a cartoon character!" said Dooley with a laugh.

"Who cares? I want to be Céline because I like Céline."

"Maybe you should just be Harriet," I said. "After all, there can only be one Harriet, just like there can only be one Céline. You don't want to be a clone of another person, Harriet. You want to be yourself, right?"

Harriet gave me a smile. "Well put, Max. I like that. Okay, so maybe I'll be Harriet. It's not a bad name, as names go."

We had left the police station, where Odelia decided to join her husband in his office to discuss the case and the fallout from the illegal search of the victim's brother's hotel room. Gran and Scarlett had decided to retire to their usual spot at the Star Hotel for a cappuccino and a hot chocolate with extra whipped cream and chocolate sprinkles, and the four of us were happy to be out of Uncle Alec's office, where the atmosphere had been a little too tense for our liking. We'd never seen the Chief so upset, though I guess he had every right to be. It's not every day that your entire department is being sued by a prominent law firm, as well as the Chief's niece, his mother, and his mother's friend. I had the impression that Eric Ross was even going to sue us, though I very much doubted he could make that stick.

"Okay, so where does this all leave us?" asked Harriet. "Who killed Robert Ross and why? We have a case to solve, you guys, or next time we see Odelia, Gran, and Scarlett, it will be in the prison visiting room."

We had been traipsing along and now found ourselves in nearby Hampton Cove Park, where we paused next to a bench. On top of the bench, a homeless person lay, looking very much in need of a shave and a bath. So we decided to position ourselves upwind from the man and hold an impromptu action meeting. Though it could have been a strategy meeting, of course. I'm not management material, so I'm not up to date on their funny lingo.

"Okay, so let's look at the facts," I told my friends. "Early this morning, Robert asks Captain Gerard to tell the crew to leave the Aurora. They assume he's expecting a special guest and wants to be alone with them. The night before, he had a visit from Sebastian Poe, the man he assumed he accidentally killed a couple of weeks ago. Poe and Robert decide to let bygones be bygones, especially since Poe is about to get married to the daughter of the tribal chief who saved his life. Robert gives him all the money that's in his safe as well as some of his so-called candy, and Poe goes on his way, possibly carjacking Chantal Jones's car in the process."

"But why?" asked Harriet.

"We'll have to ask Poe when we find him."

"He shouldn't have done it," said Dooley. "Now that he's getting married to the love of his life, it's going to mean bad karma for the poor man."

I wasn't all that sanguine that this daughter of the tribal chief was the love of Poe's life but decided not to dwell on the topic. "So at ten o'clock, someone sneaks aboard the Aurora, either by swimming over or by using a dinghy or rowing boat. The killer and Robert must have known each other, and possibly this is the person he had planned to meet, for the killer manages to put cyanide in Robert's soda, and the actor ends up drinking the whole can."

"He could have been forced to drink it," Brutus pointed out.

"It's possible," I agreed, "that he drank that soda at gunpoint. Death must have happened within minutes, at which point the killer shoved Robert's body into the pool and left. The next person on the scene, as far as we know, was Odelia."

"So who did it, Max?" asked Brutus. "Suzanne Palmer, like

Flame seems to think? Or another member of the crew? Have their whereabouts been confirmed?"

"They have," I said. "Captain Gerard went to the spa while the rest of his crew went shopping in town, and Suzanne Palmer was one of them. She says she was with Jeanine Bishop the entire time, though of course they could be supplying each other with an alibi. They certainly had their reasons for murdering Robert, since the man had attacked Suzanne. And because of that, one of the other crew members could also have done the deed, figuring Robert didn't deserve to live after the way he had treated them all, and especially Suzanne. Marcus, especially, may have had his own reasons."

"Why?" asked Brutus. "I thought he was Robert's personal stooge?"

"That's what everyone thought, but Robert stabbed his so-called stooge in the back when he denied him the role of villain in his next James Fox movie. Marcus was so upset that he went and told the production company behind the movie franchise what kind of a man their star actor really was. He told them all about the parties, the drugs, and the rest of it, though he may have left out the Sebastian Poe incident, as that would have implicated himself as well."

"Okay, so Suzanne and Marcus," said Brutus. "Who else?"

"Captain Gerard wasn't happy with the way things were going on the Aurora. He hadn't signed up for the kind of trip Robert had taken him and his crew on. If word ever got out about what was going on, Gerard might be tainted by association and lose both his sterling reputation and his career."

"Gran seems to think that Eric Ross killed his brother," said Dooley.

"It's possible," I said, "but unlikely. Eric wasn't in town when his brother died. He was in his office in Cincinnati, where his secretary has already confirmed his presence. So unless she's lying, which is possible, of course, he probably isn't our guy."

"Which only leaves Sebastian Poe," said Brutus. "And I think he's our man."

A whiff of a particularly bad odor tickled our nostrils and made us wrinkle our noses. When we looked up, we saw that the vagrant was sitting up and drinking from a bottle. Apparently, our yapping had interrupted his slumber, and he decided to have a drink. Though when I looked a little closer, I suddenly thought I recognized the man from the pictures I'd seen in Chase's office. If I wasn't mistaken, and I didn't think I was, this was Sebastian Poe!

CHAPTER 27

*O*delia had been discussing the Ross case with her
husband in his office when word reached them that
Chantal Jones's car had been found. Apparently, the carjacker
hadn't gotten far and had crashed the car into a bridge abut-
ment on his way out of town. The car was totaled, and there
was no trace of the carjacker. However, they had found some
cash under the seat of the car, along with a couple of small
plastic baggies containing pills. The pills matched the ones
found in Robert's suite aboard the yacht, so it was highly
likely that the carjacker was indeed the actor's old friend,
Poe, presumed dead but very much alive.

Just as Chase got off the phone, Brutus suddenly popped
in through the open window, out of breath, and said, "Poe is
in the park! The others are keeping an eye out in case he
escapes!"

Brutus had been tasked by his friends to race to the police
station and alert them of Poe's presence in the park. Without
wasting time, Odelia and Chase hurried out of the station,
jumped into Chase's squad car, and raced over to the park to
apprehend the wayward former real estate broker.

As Brutus had said, the man was sitting on a park bench, drinking from a liquor bottle, and appearing very much out of it. He didn't seem injured, but then again, a man who can survive being hit over the head with a bottle and nearly drowning in the Atlantic is likely impervious to injury.

He didn't resist arrest and even seemed content to be taken into custody. As Chase led him into one of the interview rooms, he asked Odelia to join, and she gladly accepted. If they could establish that Poe had killed his friend, they could close the case and appease Eric Ross.

By the time they sat down with the Miami native, he had sobered up a little, though he still appeared worse for wear.

"So, what can you tell us about what happened this morning, Mr. Poe?" asked Chase.

The man stared at them with vacant eyes, a slight smile on his face. "I don't want to marry her, you know," he said. "I mean, am I grateful that they saved my life? Sure. But I can't marry the woman. I don't love her. And besides, I already have a girl back home." He burst into tears, and Odelia handed him a box of tissues. He gratefully took one from the dispenser and blew his nose noisily.

"So, about this morning," Chase tried again.

"I mean, it's not as if she's ugly. She's not. Tilla is actually very pretty, but I don't love her. And besides, that baby isn't mine. I'm pretty sure I never slept with her, so how can I be the father of her baby? Morton is crazy if he thinks I'm going to be coerced into a loveless marriage." He sighed deeply. "Now if only Robert hadn't knocked me off that boat, I wouldn't have ended up on the island in the first place, and they wouldn't have been able to frame me into marrying the woman."

"How can they force you to marry the woman when you're here in Hampton Cove and she's over there on her island?" asked Odelia.

"Because they're watching me," said Poe darkly. "They're watching me everywhere I go."

"You mean someone has followed you here?"

"They don't need to follow me in a physical sense. They've got eyes that can see everywhere. I can fly to the moon, and they will still be able to see me. And if I don't do as they say—zap! That's it. I'm dead."

"What do you mean, you're dead?"

"I've seen them do it. I once saw the chief kill a chicken on the other side of the island. I was with the chicken, and I saw it suddenly drop dead. And then moments later, he revived it, just like that. With the power of his mind!"

"Who? This chief you mention?"

"Chief Morton, yeah. So if he wanted to, he could do the same thing to me that he did to that chicken. One moment I'm fine, and the next, dead!"

"Okay, Poe," said Chase. "Let's try to focus on the real world, shall we? What happened last night between you and Robert? And why did you take that car?"

"I'm pretty sure he can see me now," said Poe and glanced all around the room intently, looking for a sign of the tribal leader.

Chase slapped the table with his fist. "Poe, focus!"

The man jumped. "What? Who are you?"

"Chase Kingsley. Detective in charge of the investigation into the murder of your friend, Robert Ross."

Poe's face crumpled like a used tissue, and he burst into tears. "I liked Robert. I loved him like a brother. Why did he have to hit me with that bottle? If he hadn't, I wouldn't be under the spell of that madman!" Odelia shared a look with her husband. Clearly, Sebastian Poe was in no fit state of mind to be interviewed. They were just about to end the session when the man piped up, "I didn't kill him, you know. I loved him, and he loved me. He said so himself last night.

He said he was sorry for what he did to me, and he also said he would make sure Morton wouldn't be able to touch me. And when I asked him how he thought he would accomplish that, he said he was James Fox and he slayed villains for a living. Funny guy."

"So what happened last night?" asked Chase. "Why did you take that car?"

"Well, I needed one," said Poe simply. "So I took it. And then, of course, that stupid car drove into a bridge, so I figured it was a sign from Chief Morton that my work here wasn't finished yet and that I should stick around. So I decided to hang around until I got another sign that it was time to go. And now I'm here."

"Now you're here," Odelia confirmed. "And where were you this morning, Sebastian? More specifically, at ten o'clock?"

"Um... probably asleep? I've been very tired lately. It's my head, you see. My head isn't okay."

Now, that was an understatement, Odelia thought. "So where were you asleep, Sebastian?"

"The park. I slept there last night. Did you know that park is full of cats? You wouldn't believe the noise they make. Screeching and caterwauling all night. It's terrible. I didn't sleep a wink. Terrible, terrible noise. You should do something about those cats. Get rid of them if I were you."

Odelia had taken pity on the man, but these words irked her to such an extent that she decided to become a little more forceful with him. "Did you kill your friend, Sebastian? Did you kill Robert?"

The man stared at them with big eyes. "Kill Robert? But why? I loved the guy! And he—"

"Loved you," said Chase. "Yeah, you said that." He sighed. "Look, I think you should get yourself checked out by a doctor, Sebastian. That hit on the head clearly hasn't done you any favors. And your stay on the island hasn't either. You have a girlfriend at home and a family who have been worried sick about you, so why don't you give them a call? Tell them you were lost but now you've been found."

"But I can't! Chief Morton will zap me—just like he did with that chicken."

"We'll protect you," Chase promised. "We also have secret powers here in Hampton Cove, you see. So we'll protect you from this Chief Morton."

"Secret powers? How?"

Chase turned to his wife. "Odelia here is a witch."

The man stared at Odelia in wide-eyed wonder. "A witch? Really?"

Odelia smiled. "It's true. I have witchy powers. I can talk to cats, for instance."

"Really?"

She nodded. And on her instigation, Chase opened the door, and her four cats walked in. She proceeded to exchange a few words with them, much to Sebastian's amazement.

So she waved her hands in front of the man's face, said a few incantations she made up on the spot, and finally said he was free from Morton's curse and could go home a free man.

"My God," said Sebastian. "You're right. I suddenly feel so light. You have freed me!" And to show his gratitude, he actually hugged her. Which wasn't such a pleasant experience since he was very smelly.

A police officer escorted the man out, after receiving instructions to take Sebastian to the nearest hospital and get him a phone so he could call his family in Miami.

The moment he was gone, she asked, "Are you sure this won't come back to bite us in the ass, babe?"

"I'm pretty sure it won't. The guy is completely out of it."

"Yeah, but still."

"So what if he tells people that you can talk to cats? Who's going to believe him?"

"Are you just going to let him walk?" asked Brutus. "He could be Robert's killer."

"I very much doubt it," said Odelia. "I think what Sebastian Poe needs right now is not a lengthy prison sentence but a prolonged stay at the hospital."

"At the very least, you should arrest him for carjacking," said Harriet.

"He's not going anywhere," said Odelia. "We'll put an officer at the hospital to keep an eye on him. In due course, he'll have to face the music for last night's carjacking and for assaulting Chantal, but right now, we'll make sure he sobers up and gets well again."

Which is when their next interviewee was brought in by Sarah Flunk, who had picked the man up at his hotel. Marcus O'Reilly sat down across from them and already looked a lot less cocky than he had before. And when they confronted him with the allegations, he grabbed a tissue and burst into tears.

CHAPTER 28

I have to say, I felt a little bit sorry for Marcus as he sat blubbering in the interview room. And it didn't take long before he confessed to what he'd done. "It's true," he said as he sniffled freely. "I did it. I sent an anonymous email to the producers of the James Fox movies that Robert Ross was a terrible human being, an addict, and was abusive with women. I was angry and I lashed out, and I realize I shouldn't have done it, but I did, and I'm so sorry!"

"You thought you were going to be the next James Fox villain," said Chase, "and when you found out that Robert had lied to you, you decided to get even."

Marcus nodded. "He had built my hopes up, and then he just squashed them again, just because he could. I had already told all of my friends, my parents. My dad was so proud of me. He said he'd buy tickets for the whole family, and they'd all go and see the movie together. And now I had to tell them it wasn't going to happen. It was so humiliating."

"And so you decided to get even."

"I did! Oh, I so did!"

"So you killed him."

There was a beat, then Marcus gaped at the cop. "Wait, what?"

"You were so angry with Robert for lying to you that you killed him. You poisoned his can of soda and fed it to him, and then you watched him die."

"Like a true Fox villain would," Dooley added for good measure.

"No!" said Marcus. "I sent that email, but I didn't kill the guy."

"Do you really want us to believe that, Marcus? After you lied to us before?"

"Okay, so I lied, but that's just because... because..."

Chase was leaning forward, his eyes boring into Marcus's. Then he pounded the table with his fist, causing us all to jump. "Because you killed him! Admit it!"

"No, I didn't! I just didn't want my bosses to know what I'd done. I could get in some serious trouble if they knew I'd been emailing people about a client. They could terminate my contract, and then I'd never work in the industry again. So of course I didn't tell anyone about what I did. I'd be crazy if I did."

"So where were you this morning at ten, Marcus?"

"Like I already told you, I went shopping. Look, if you want to find out who killed Robert, ask Gerard. He's the one who kept having to cover up for Robert. If the company found out about what was going on the Aurora, it was his career on the line. I could always find a different job in a different line of work. But Gerard? He only had a couple of years more to go, and then he'd get a nice fat pension. But if he got canned now? No career but also no pension. That man had a lot more to lose than I did if Robert kept behaving the way he did."

. . .

WHICH WAS VERY convenient since our next interviewee was Captain Jean-Luc Gerard himself. He, too, looked a lot less self-assured than he had been that morning. When confronted with the allegations Marcus had leveled against him, he folded like a cheap suit. "Okay, I admit it, being in charge of the Aurora with Robert Ross as our client was a major headache for all of us, but mostly for me. If the yacht company found out there was drug abuse, women being assaulted, and a man being murdered and chucked over-board, I would have lost the pension that I'd worked thirty years to build up, it's true. But that doesn't mean I killed him. I mean, if I had, and I was seen, that would have been the end of my life, not just my career. So I didn't touch the guy. All I could hope for was that our trip would end soon."

"So why didn't you ask that someone else take over from you?" asked Chase.

"It's not that easy. I would have had to give a good reason."

"Health reasons."

"That would have ended my career. If I was too sick to captain the Aurora, I was too sick to captain any ship, and they would have let me go. No, I couldn't do that. And also, if a different captain was put in charge, how long do you think it would have been before they realized what kind of a guy Robert Ross was? My replacement may have even heard rumors about what happened to Poe. And then it would all come back to me."

"So you decided to stay and ride out the storm."

"Something like that."

"But you have to admit that Robert being murdered suits you very well, Captain Gerard," said Odelia.

"Oh, I'm not denying that his death came at an opportune time for all of us. Though now with everything coming out in the open, I'm not sure how much good it will do us. I already got an official missive from the yacht company that their lawyers want to talk to us. It doesn't bode well for our future."

I couldn't imagine it would. If word got out about the things that had taken place on the yacht, it was the company's reputation on the line, and so they'd probably try to use the captain and his crew as scapegoats and throw them to the wolves. However way you looked at it, things didn't look so good for Captain Gerard. And the man knew it, for he looked decidedly unhappy.

"Look, I had nothing to do with the man's death. Like I said, I spent all morning at the spa. I figured I deserved a treat. Ask anyone. They'll confirm I was there."

"We checked," said Chase. "And while they confirm that you booked the spa and arrived there, they can't confirm you were there all the time."

"Oh, for crying out loud. I didn't like the guy, but I didn't kill him!"

"That's what they all say," Brutus grunted. And wasn't that the truth?

THE NEXT PERSON TO take the hot seat was Oliver Grant, who was none other than the late Robert Ross's agent. He was in town to assist Robert's brother in handling the actor's funeral and going through his personal belongings. I had a feeling he had also been tasked to make sure that the actor's legacy wasn't tainted by these allegations of the man's bad behavior. After all, if word got out about what kind of a man Robert really was, it would affect the movie franchise he had been the face of for the past fifteen years, to detrimental effect.

Mr. Grant was a clean-cut young man with a baby face and the aspect of a lawyer. The moment he sat down, he shot his cuffs and then patiently waited for the first question.

"He looks like a shark," Dooley commented.

"A baby-faced shark," said Brutus. "The most dangerous kind."

"Why is that, Brutus?" asked Dooley.

"Because you never see them coming, Dooley."

"So, is it true that your client was being fired as James Fox, Mr. Grant?" asked Chase.

The man laughed a very fake laugh. "Who told you that? Of course he wasn't being fired. He was the best Fox we ever had. He made the studio billions. If anything, they were begging him to add another three movies, making him the actor with the most Fox movies in history. It would have turned Robert Ross into a legend on par with—what's this?" He quickly scanned the email Chase had placed before him, and his face clouded. Then his lips formed a perfect O.

"It's the email Robert sent his brother," Chase clarified, in case it wasn't clear.

The agent shoved the document away from him as if it had personally insulted him. "Hearsay," he blustered.

"You'll find that the original email the producers sent to your client was added to the email he sent to his brother. We talked to the producers, and they have confirmed that they were severing all ties with the actor. They weren't happy with the behavior he had displayed, which reflected badly on them and on their billion-dollar franchise. In fact, they were lawyering up and were going to sue Robert for breach of contract, most notably the infamous morality clause in his contract, of which I'm sure you're well aware, Mr. Grant. As his agent, you negotiated his contracts, so you knew perfectly well that Robert was in breach."

The agent dusted a piece of imaginary fluff off the table. "They officially confirmed all this? In writing?"

"They did." Chase shoved another email in front of the agent, who read it intently. Finally, he sat back, and I could see his mind working overtime.

"Okay, so that's their prerogative," he said. "I'll have to talk to our lawyers about this, but if this is their official position..."

"Look, I don't really care about the company's beef with your client," said Chase. "All I care about is that you were being put in a very difficult position. If Robert was fired from the franchise, that wouldn't go down well with your bosses at the agency. You might even lose your own job in the aftermath."

"They would never do that. I have other clients. I'm a valuable asset."

"Robert Ross was your most prominent client. If you lost him..."

The man looked thoroughly annoyed, and I had the impression that Chase was getting to him. "Okay, look. So I wasn't happy about the whole situation. None of us were. But we were dealing with it, all right?"

"And how were you 'dealing' with it, Mr. Grant?"

"Is that the reason you flew in from LA last night?" asked Odelia. "To deal with the fallout from Robert's increasingly outrageous behavior and drug abuse?"

"There's nobody who appreciates more than me what Robert has meant for the agency—for the movie industry at large, in fact. But it is true that lately his behavior was getting out of control. And so when I heard about the incident with the girl—"

"Suzanne Palmer?"

The agent nodded. "That was the last straw. When we were told—"

"Who told you?"

"I don't think it's relevant who—"

"Who told you!" Chase insisted.

His eyes shot across the room like a pinball machine, but finally, he murmured, "Miss Palmer's friend."

"Jeanine Bishop?"

He nodded. "She called me personally. Said her friend had been involved in an altercation. Apparently, Robert had attacked her, and she had taken a swing at the guy. So I confronted him over the phone, and he admitted the whole thing. Which is when we held a meeting at the agency and decided that something needed to be done. Some of us felt we needed to cut him loose, while others insisted on keeping him on board and..." He hesitated and leaned forward. "Can I talk to you guys off the record for a moment?"

"This is a murder inquiry, Mr. Grant," Chase pointed out. "There is no 'off the record,' I'm afraid."

The agent clammed up for a moment, then decided to forge ahead. "Okay, so they sent me here to talk to Miss Palmer. To convince her..."

"Not to mention what happened to anyone?"

The agent nodded unhappily.

"And to offer her money in exchange for her silence, maybe?"

Again he nodded.

"And if she said no?"

"Then we'd have no other recourse than to fire our client. And if I'd known that the producers had already fired him, I probably could have stayed home and not bothered to fly out here."

"I thought you were here to help with the funeral arrangements?"

"That's not my problem," said the agent. "His family will deal with that."

"So I take it you have decided to wash your hands of Mr. Ross?"

"Look, it's not my fault that the guy went off the reservation. I mean, my God, drugs and murder and assaulting women? We don't condone that kind of behavior."

"So you've heard about Sebastian Poe, have you?" asked Odelia.

"Yeah, Miss Bishop told us about that as well. Though I have to admit it all sounded a little... too much, even for a guy like Ross. But I checked, and it's true that Poe disappeared a couple of weeks ago. I talked to his girlfriend, and he left on his yacht one morning and never came back. And it's true that Poe and Ross were thick as thieves, so..."

"Poe didn't die," said Chase reluctantly. Clearly, he enjoyed watching the agent squirm.

The agent sat up with a jerk. "He's alive?"

"He is. We talked to him just now, and he will be fine."

"Oh, that's great news!" he said. He grabbed his phone. "Do you mind if I send off a quick message?"

"Yes, I do," said Chase curtly, dampening the agent's excitement to some degree. But it was clear that the man felt he'd been given a new lease on life.

"I have the impression that the only reason they decided to cut Robert loose is not because he took drugs or attacked Suzanne," said Harriet, "but because they thought he killed his friend."

"Yeah, I also get that impression," I agreed. "And the only reason Mr. Grant is in Hampton Cove is to try and bury both stories once and for all."

"Nasty little man," Brutus said, and I couldn't help but concur.

CHAPTER 29

The round of interviews was over, and so we decided to get some fresh air. Brutus and Harriet wanted to return home and see if their litter boxes had been filled again, and Dooley and I wandered over to the General Store to give an update on the case to Kingman, who had expressed an interest. As a big fan of the James Fox movies, he wanted to be kept in the loop. Which is why we soon found ourselves in the pleasant company of our voluminous friend, who was snacking on a tasty new sampling of kibble when we joined him.

"I'm not sure what's in this," he told us, "but it's not bad, not bad at all. Have a taste, fellas, and tell me what you think."

And so we tucked in, which wasn't exactly a great hardship, as the kibble certainly was tasty enough. "I like it," said Dooley. "It tastes like... chicken?"

"Fish, I'd say," I said as I rolled a piece of kibble around in my mouth.

"Beef jerky," said Kingman. "It's got this really punchy aftertaste."

And since we couldn't agree, we decided to ask Clarice, who just happened to pass by at that moment. She didn't say no to a free bowl of kibble, but after she had dug her teeth in, she flashed us a big grin. "I don't think you're going to like this, fellas."

"Why? What's wrong with it?" asked Kingman with a touch of concern.

"It's rat," said Clarice. "And I also taste some black beetle in there, and if I'm not mistaken, some cockroach too. And chicken," she said in deference to Dooley. "I'd say that this here kibble was made in a factory under not very sanitary conditions. They should probably add a label that says, 'May contain traces of rat, black beetle and cockroach.'"

"Yikes!" Kingman cried and immediately started upchucking the previously delicious kibble he'd imbibed. And since, like yawning, vomiting is contagious, Dooley and I did the same thing.

So when Kingman's human, Wilbur Vickery, came walking out of the store, attracted by the unmistakable sound of three cats vomiting, he stared down at us with his hands on his hips for a moment, then picked up the bowl of kibble, shook his head, and said, "I should have known it was garbage. Thanks, Kingman. I'll send it back to the supplier."

"He's using us as guinea pigs!" Dooley cried, not looking all that happy.

"Why do you think he keeps feeding us this stuff?" asked Kingman, removing a piece of rat/beetle/cockroach kibble from between his teeth. "He wants us to try it first, and then if we don't like it, he won't sell it."

"I like it," said Clarice, who looked disappointed that Wilbur had removed the bowl. "For a refined palate like mine, it hits the spot."

"It hit my spot also," said Kingman, pointing to his stomach. "A little too hard, though."

"Rat is good for you," said Clarice. "Nice succulent meat. And beetles and cockroaches are full of proteins and contain everything a growing kitty needs. So I don't see why you guys are complaining."

"I'm allergic to cockroaches," said Kingman. "And beetles. And rats."

"How can you be allergic to something you've never eaten?" Clarice cried.

"I ate it now, and I'm allergic," said Kingman, pointing to the little puddle at his paws.

"Wilbur should never have offered us this kibble," said Dooley. "It's not what a true cat daddy does."

"And what does a true cat daddy do?" asked Clarice with a slight grin.

"Well, he makes sure that his cats always get the food they need, but also the food they can easily digest, and he doesn't try to poison them with this stuff that's full of horrible things like beetles and cockroaches and rats."

"Yeah, even if he has to taste the food himself first to make sure it's kosher," Kingman chimed in, "he'll gladly make that sacrifice because that's what a true cat daddy does. Isn't it so, Dooley?"

"Absolutely," Dooley confirmed.

Clarice chuckled. "You guys are delusional."

I have to admit I only heard snatches of this last piece of conversation, for my mind had suddenly started spinning in overdrive. "Could you repeat that last bit, Kingman?" I asked.

"About a true cat daddy? Sure. He saves the food from his own lips to feed his beloved precious cat, that's what he does. It's all about sacrifice, Max."

"That's it!" I cried, pointing at our friend. "You just solved a murder!"

"I did?" asked Kingman, much surprised. But then he

smiled. "Of course I did. Because I'm that clever." Then he frowned. "So who did it, Max?"

* * *

BERT COLLINS WAS WORKING alongside his wife in the lovely little garden they had created behind the house. It was Jane's pride and joy, along with her designs, of course. Even the kids had enjoyed spending time in the backyard when they were little, though now that they were bigger, they hadn't set foot in it for years, except when Bert took out his barbecue and organized one of his famous feasts. That hadn't happened in a little while, though, since Jane hadn't been feeling so great lately, so it was deemed best if they didn't have friends over for a little while until she felt up to meeting people again.

He didn't think it would be long before she emerged from her most recent slump, though. Especially now that her former boyfriend had died. The story would be all over the news, of course, but eventually, the hubbub would die down, and then the man would finally be out of their lives forever. Bert just hoped the police wouldn't drop by again with their questions and their annoying habit of digging into the past and dragging it all up again. He hoped he had made that clear to them. Which is why he was so surprised when he looked up and saw that Detective Kingsley was staring down at him, and also Mrs. Kingsley. They were accompanied by their cats, as usual, which struck him as weird and slightly unsettling.

He got up with some effort and hoped Jane hadn't noticed the arrival of the detecting duo. Which is why he hurried to join them and invite them into the house, where Jane wouldn't see them.

"I thought I told you not to bother us anymore?" he whispered as he ushered them into the house.

"That was before we realized what you did, Mr. Collins," said Detective Kingsley.

His blood suddenly turned to ice in his veins. It couldn't be. But when he looked into the man's eyes, he saw that he knew. But how?

But then, since he had decided long ago that when the police ever came knocking on his door accusing him of a crime he had, in fact, committed, that he would immediately confess, since he wasn't the kind of person who could remain firm under pressure, he heaved a deep sigh.

"How did you know?" he simply asked.

CHAPTER 30

❧

*O*nce again, we sat in Chase's squad car as the cop drove along with Mr. Collins in the back. Only this time, he was taking the man into custody. Odelia had decided to stay behind to be with Mrs. Collins and to wait until her sister arrived to take care of the woman and the kids while Bert was being processed and interrogated. But apparently, he didn't want to wait that long because the moment he stepped into the car, he started telling us the whole story.

"He should never have come back here," he said. "The moment I found out about it, I knew what the impact on Jane would be. She never stopped loving him, you see. And sometimes I even think that the whole reason she's suffered so much is because of what he did to her. Nobody knows about this apart from myself and, of course, Jane herself, but he actually got her pregnant, and then when she told him, he decided that he didn't want the kid and walked out on her. She lost the baby, possibly due to the severe depression she fell into when he broke up with her. But somehow she still managed to get through all that, but the truth was that she developed a sort of obsession with the guy. In spite of what he did to her and the cruel way he treated her, she loved him, and that never stopped."

"You don't have to tell me all this, sir," said Chase. "It's better to wait until we're at the police station."

"It's fine. I just want to get it off my chest, if you don't mind. When I met Jane, she was twenty-three, and quite possibly the most beautiful and lovely girl I had ever met. I fell in love with her at first glance, and at first, she seemed interested in me as well, so I thought I'd struck gold, you know, mutual attraction. Love at first sight and all that. Before long, we started dating, and that's when I realized that Jane wasn't capable of loving anyone other than the man who had broken her heart. And her heart wasn't the only thing he had broken, for even though she seemed happy and outgoing and sweet and kind, deep down she was incapable of being truly, unreservedly happy. And she was definitely incapable of loving anyone, and certainly not me. But I didn't mind. I just figured I had enough love for the both of us, which maybe I had, and maybe I hadn't. So when I proposed and she said yes, I thought it was the start of something terrific. It took her a couple of years to trust me enough to tell me what had happened to her. I still remember as if it was yesterday. We were watching a James Fox movie, and she suddenly burst into tears, big, loud sobs. When I asked her what was going on, she refused to tell me. When I insisted, it all came out. Which is when a lot of things suddenly fell into place. At my instigation, she started seeing a psychiatrist, and that helped a lot, I have to say. After all, we had four beautiful daughters together and, on the whole, have led a blessed life. But Jane is still broken, even after all those years, and I've had to accept that."

"What a story, Max," said Dooley.

"Yeah, what a story," I agreed.

"So James Fox movies were banned in our house, and I put a block on the name Robert Ross on our computers and our phones to make sure Jane would never be confronted with that man ever again. And we were lucky for a long time in that he wasn't interested in her. Not one little bit. Until last week, when he suddenly announced out of the blue that he was arriving in Hampton Cove and wouldn't she like to meet up, for old time's sake? She didn't tell me about it, knowing how I would react. But I found out anyway when I saw her googling the guy on one of our daughters' phones. It wasn't hard to find out he had been traveling around on his yacht, the Aurora, and that his travels were taking him to Hampton Cove, where he was being celebrated by the Chamber of Commerce. One of Jane's best friends is Caroline Poots, you see. If she'd known about what that man did to Jane, she probably would never have invited him. But then, like I said, nobody knew apart from me and Jane. She hadn't even told her parents. And so when she snuck out of the house a couple of days ago, I decided to follow her. It wasn't a big surprise to find that she took a cab to the marina, where she boarded the Aurora. I don't know what he told her, but that evening she was even more distant and emotionally reserved than usual. Like I said, she never stopped loving him, and even though I don't know for sure, I can only guess that he fed her a lot of nonsense about getting back together and rekindling their romance. Guys like Robert Ross often start thinking about their past, and regrets about the things they did or didn't do makes them maudlin and sentimental. They regret not having raised a family. And then they remember some old girlfriend and the baby she told him she was expecting. It's even possible that she told Ross that one of our daughters was actually his and decided to hide the ugly truth."

"I don't think I will watch his movies anymore, Max," said Dooley.

"I think a lot of people won't watch them after the truth comes out, Dooley."

"I knew she was going to meet him again," said Bert. "She was happy, all of a sudden. Bouncy, even. As if she was in love—butterflies in her stomach. But I knew he'd break her heart again. Men like Ross are incapable of loving anyone other than themselves. He was setting her up to be disappointed all over again, and this time she might not survive. So I decided to put a stop to her torment once and for all. To put a stop to her tormentor. Because I do love my wife. For real, not because I'm feeling restless and want to indulge in some fantasy for a while, until I'm bored with her and cast her away again. I knew she was going to see him at eleven o'clock this morning because she had been to the hair salon and had bought a new dress and said she was meeting Caroline in town. She had even marked it in her calendar. But when I called Caroline under some pretext and mentioned the meeting, she obviously had no idea what I was talking about.

"I figured that Ross would probably be alone for his big date. He wouldn't want anybody spoiling the fun. So I drove down to the marina, took one of the dinghies that are always moored there, and rowed over to the Aurora. I checked to see if the coast was clear, then climbed on board and simply walked up to the man. To say he was surprised to see me would be an understatement. But I quickly made it clear I meant him no harm, and when I explained I was Jane's husband, he calmed down. I said I wanted to talk to him man to man and wanted to know what his intentions were. I think he was greatly amused by that and decided he liked this game and wanted to have a little fun with me. So he offered me a drink and got one out for himself. I knew he loved his

Dr. Pepper Cotton Candy, so that's what I asked for. Then, when he wasn't looking, I simply dumped the cyanide into the can and made the switch. He never noticed, too busy as he was telling me all about how he had never stopped loving Jane and that he felt they deserved a second chance. He also told me that Jane had confessed she wasn't happy with me. I have to admit that stung, but then I remembered that Jane wasn't happy, period, and probably would never be happy again—ever. She was that broken."

"Where did you get the cyanide?" asked Chase.

"I had it in the shed, behind lock and key, of course. Got it from my dad, who was a farmer and bought it years ago to kill rabbits on his farm. So I figured I'd finally put it to good use."

"So you put it in his soda, and then you watched him die."

"Then I watched him die," Bert confirmed. "And I have to say, it didn't give me great pleasure. I loved his movies, Detective Kingsley. And I thought he was a great actor but a terrible human being. But if my wife was going to live, Ross had to die."

"And then you dumped his body in the pool."

"I figured you'd probably see through it, but I did it anyway. At the very least, I'd buy myself a couple of hours while you figured he'd drowned."

"We saw through it in minutes," Chase grunted.

"Which just goes to show what a lousy murderer I am," said Bert ruefully.

"So how did you stop Jane from meeting the guy at eleven?"

"Simple. I had bought one of those unregistered phones and sent her a message pretending to be Ross and claiming that I'd lost my phone and postponing the meeting. I hoped she would buy the deceit, and she did."

"You could have sent that message from Ross's phone."

"Yes, but then you would have immediately established a link between my wife and the dead man. And that's the last thing I wanted. Actually, I had hoped you would leave us out of the whole thing entirely. After all, it was twenty-five years ago."

"When a famous actor returns to his home town after twenty-five years only to end up being murdered, it's only natural that we start looking into possible ties between the victim and the town. And so your wife's name cropped up."

"I hope this won't affect her too much," said Bert. "I mean, she won't miss me, not in a romantic sense. But she will suffer from the disruption in her daily routine. And so she'll probably miss me in a practical sense."

"Maybe in her own way, she does love you, Mr. Collins."

The man smiled. "I would like very much to believe that, detective. I really would."

CHAPTER 31

We were enjoying one of those rare moments of familial bliss in our backyard, with Tex manning the grill and the entire family gathered for the feast, when Dooley raised the alarm. "Max! Our litter! It's gone again!"

Immediately, we jumped down from the swing and followed our friend into the house. And it was as he had predicted: Harriet and Brutus's litter boxes were once again devoid of their usual littery contents. Only that morning, Marge had filled them up again after we had pointed out the dreadful dearth to her, and now the precious substance had once again disappeared without a trace.

And since at heart we're scientists, and no statement is relevant without a second opinion, we hurried out of Marge and Tex's house and over to Odelia and Chase's dwelling, where unfortunately the same unsettling sight met our eyes: our litter boxes were also empty, even though Odelia had followed her mother's example and had filled them up that morning.

"This isn't happening!" Brutus cried, much dismayed.

"I told you that the litter monster is on the move," said Dooley. "Didn't I tell you?"

"There is no such thing as a litter monster, Dooley," I felt obliged to point out.

"There is a cookie monster, Max," he said. "So there is bound to be a litter monster as well. A monster who likes to eat litter and simply can't get enough of the stuff."

Loathe as I was to accept that this might be true, maybe he had a point. Why else would our litter keep disappearing? It wasn't because our humans had been struck by the desire to economize since they had decided not to skimp on litter and had gotten us one of the best brands this time, to reward us for the role we had played in the capture of Mr. Ross's murderer and also because we had had to do without litter for a while.

"Okay, so we need to figure this out," I told my friends. "And the only way we can is by laying a trap."

"A mouse trap?" asked Dooley. But then he got it. "Ooh, I see what you mean! A litter monster trap!"

"Better build a big trap," Brutus grunted. "Because a monster that can eat four trays of litter must be huge."

And so it was decided. Odelia would fill up the litter box once again, we would all pretend to be next door, enjoying our barbecue, while in actual fact, one of us would stay behind, carefully concealed, and catch this monster in the act of absconding with this vital ingredient to a cat's happy home life. And since it was my idea in the first place, I was selected as the hapless volunteer.

Odelia was alerted to the terrible tragedy that had befallen her cat contingent, the ruse was created, the trap set, and so while the others all enjoyed their food, I hid underneath the couch, from where I had a good view of the kitchen, where our litter boxes stood in the small alcove behind the fridge. I hoped it wouldn't be long before the thief showed up because my stomach was rumbling, and I wouldn't have minded a bite to eat.

I had kept my eye on the prize when all of a sudden the pet flap moved. But when I was ready to spring, I saw that it was Dooley.

"Max? Where are you?" he whispered.

"Over here!" I said, and he joined me underneath the couch.

"Nice and cozy, isn't it?" he said.

"Well..." I glanced over. "Did you bring me something to eat?"

"No, I didn't. I just figured you'd get lonely, so I decided to keep you company."

The sentiment was noble, but the lack of food still rankled. And so we waited. And waited. And waited.

"So how did you find out that Bert Collins killed Robert Ross, Max?" Dooley finally asked, boredom starting to hold him in its grip.

"Something Kingman said about sacrifice. And also the fact that he's allergic to cockroaches."

"Is Bert Collins also allergic to cockroaches, you think?"

I smiled. "No, but Jane Collins is allergic to dogs, remember? Which is why Robert asked one of his crew members to walk Flame while he was entertaining his old girlfriend. I'd been wondering why he would do that since he truly loved that dog. So why would he send her off the boat? It could only be because his visitor had expressed a fervent wish not to be in the presence of the dog. And then when Jane told us she was allergic to dogs, it didn't register at first, but then suddenly when we were chatting with Kingman about cockroaches, it did."

"Jane could have killed Robert and not Bert."

"Yes, that's where the sacrifice came in. Jane could never kill Robert. She loved him and had loved him from the

194

beginning. She lied about their break-up having been a natural consequence of their lives drifting apart. Her feelings for the man were a lot stronger than she admitted to us—or to her husband."

"So how did you end up with Bert being the killer?"

"Well, if Jane hadn't killed Robert, then who had? It was obvious that he was meeting her that morning, and it was also obvious that Bert loved his wife and wanted to protect her at all cost from anything that might upset her. He even made sure they didn't get the *Gazette*, though from Jane's statements we know she had read the paper that morning, presumably behind her husband's back, and to follow the news about Robert arriving in Hampton Cove first-hand. Because Bert was right about that: the news that both fascinated and upset his wife the most was anything that had to do with Robert Ross. Which is why I figured he just might be the one who killed the actor. And then when we confronted him, he quickly confessed."

"So he sacrificed himself out of love for his wife?"

"If you take the charitable view, yes, he did. Though you could also say he killed Robert because he was afraid he would steal Jane away from him. Which he just might have done if Bert hadn't interfered."

For a moment, we both ruminated on the case of the murdered mega-star, but then all of a sudden, the pet flap moved again, and we both hunkered down, ready to pounce on the litter monster. But as the kitchen door opened, we saw that it was Gran who entered. She glanced left and right, then quickly ventured in, a plastic garbage bag in hand. And as we watched, she emptied the litter boxes into the bag, hoisted it onto her back, and hurried out again.

To say we were flabbergasted would be an understatement.

"Max, the litter monster is... Gran!"

"I know. But why?"

After we had recovered sufficiently from the shock of our discovery, we ventured out through the pet door in Gran's wake. We had to find out what she was up to!

We soon caught up with her and discovered she had retreated to the safety of her beloved rose bushes, where she was busy pouring out the litter and mixing it with some of the potting soil she had apparently stored there. After she had mixed up the batch, she transferred the newly mixed soil to a bucket, then quickly carried it over to the flower beds she had recently planted and which were her pride and joy. Since neither Odelia nor Chase are blessed with green thumbs, Gran had taken it upon herself to take care of their backyard.

She now spread the mixture over the flower beds and made sure to tuck in her flowers nice and snug, covering the ground with the stuff. Then, as she glanced over her shoulder to make sure she hadn't been spotted, she hurried back to her own backyard. But when she looked back, she caught sight of the two of us, and she brought a distraught hand to her mouth.

"Max! Dooley!" she said. "How long have you been standing there?"

"Long enough to see what you did," I said, not seeing the point of beating around the bush.

"You're the litter monster, Gran," said Dooley accusingly. "But why?"

Gran sighed deeply and retraced her steps, then settled down on her haunches in front of us. "Okay, I'll tell you. But only if you promise to keep my secret, all right?"

"On one condition," I said.

"Anything."

"Please leave those poor caterpillars alone. Very soon

now, they'll all turn into beautiful butterflies, and you'll be happy that you saved their lives."

"Okay, fine. I won't touch them. See, the thing is that my flowers are suffering. Either they get too much water when it rains, like these last couple of days, or they don't get enough. And then I read that cat litter is a wonderful ingredient for creating the perfect atmosphere. It retains water and prevents plants from drying out, but it also offers the necessary drainage so the plants don't drown. In other words, the perfect ingredient to make your plants happy."

"But why steal it?" I asked. "Couldn't you just buy the stuff?"

"That's just it. Tex doesn't want me to! I told him about how great the stuff is for our plants, but he claims it's a waste of money to use expensive cat litter for gardening purposes. And so if he won't let me buy it, I decided to steal some of it instead. And it's just for the time being, you know, until my plants are strong enough to survive under any weather conditions." She got up again with a slight effort. "So now you know."

"Now we know," I agreed.

"So what are you going to tell the others?"

"I'm not sure," I admitted.

"Will you tell them the truth?"

She stared at us, and we stared right back. Now under normal circumstances, I don't take kindly to people who steal my stuff. But this was different. This was a matter of life and death—for Gran's plants. And so a plan formed in my mind.

"I'll think of something," I finally said.

She smiled a grateful smile. "After that debacle at the Star Hotel, my stock isn't trading very high at the moment, so if they find out I'm the litter thief, they might throw me in jail."

"They won't," I said. That whole fracas with Robert Ross's

NIC SAINT

brother had been dealt with by Charlene Butterwick herself. After we had caught his brother's murderer, Eric Ross had been so relieved and grateful that he had quickly decided to drop any lawsuit he might have considered bringing against us. A quiet word from the Mayor and the implicit promise of a posthumous ceremony to award the key to the city to the late actor hadn't hurt.

Though when the truth about Mr. Ross came to light, and his reputation took a hit, maybe that ceremony would be just as quietly canceled again.

We had returned to join the others, and when Odelia took a seat next to us on the swing to find out what we had found out, I told her in solemn tones that her father was the culprit. That we had seen him sneak into the house, remove the litter, and sneak out again.

"But why?" asked Odelia. "Why would Dad steal your litter?"

I pointed to the grill. "We all know that cat litter is perfect for keeping your grill clean, Odelia. You sprinkle some of it in the grill before you start cooking, and it will collect all the grease. Then once you're done, you simply remove the litter, and your grill will be clean in no time. Easy peasy. Only cat litter is expensive, and I'm sure your dad doesn't want you to know he uses it for that purpose."

Odelia smiled. "Oh, the sweetheart. Well, his secret is safe with me."

She rejoined the others and made sure to give her dad a peck on the cheek, causing the man to look up in pleasant surprise.

Moments later, Marge sat down next to us. "So who has been stealing your litter?"

"It was Odelia," I said.

"Odelia! But why?"

"Well, we all know that cat litter absorbs moisture and

bad smells. So she likes to put some of it in her closets to get rid of that musty smell. But since cat litter costs a lot of money, she didn't want to tell you."

"Oh, poor darling," said Marge, touched. "I won't betray her secret." And so she left us to return to the feast and gave her daughter a hug in the process.

Harriet and Brutus now stared at me, and also Grace. The latter asked, "So who did steal your litter, Max? And tell us the truth this time."

"It was your dad," I revealed. "We all know that cat litter is perfect for removing greasy spots. So he's been using it to get rid of those grease spots on the driveway by covering them with litter. It works like a charm."

"Oh, that's so sweet of him," said Grace and hopped off the swing to give her dad a big hug, which the cop responded to by giving her a big hug in return.

Brutus and Harriet eyed me closely, and Brutus narrowed his eyes. "I know you're lying, Max," he said. "I can tell from the way your eye twitches."

"Does my eye twitch?" I asked.

"No, it doesn't, but I still know you're lying."

"Okay, so I'll tell you the truth," I said. "But please don't tell anyone."

"Scout's honor," Brutus said.

"Cross my heart and hope to die," said Harriet.

"Okay, so you know how cat litter is great to get traction when you're driving on ice? Well, it is. So Uncle Alec decided to fill a couple of bags and put them in the trunk of his car just in case."

"But winter is months away!" said Harriet.

"Always good to be prepared, Harriet," I told her.

"I guess you're right." She glanced over at Odelia's uncle. "Oh, the poor dear. Didn't want anyone to find out that he wants us all to be safe." And so she jumped off the porch and jumped up on the Chief's lap, giving him a cuddle against his chin. Uncle Alec, who had been in the process of putting a piece of steak into his mouth, eyed her with surprise, then decided to share a piece of his meat with her.

Brutus now turned to me and whispered, "Tell me the truth, Max. The real truth this time!"

"Okay, fine. You got me," I said. "The real culprit is Scarlett. She must have read somewhere that cat litter is perfect for absorbing odors from shoes. You put some of it in an old sock, put the sock in the shoe, and voila. Almost like new."

"Genius," said Brutus, well satisfied. And so he traipsed over to Scarlett and settled on her lap.

Dooley stared at me, and I frowned. "Dooley, you know that Gran stole our litter, so don't ask me who did, all right?"

"You're such a good liar, Max. I believed you every time, even though I know the real truth—the real, real truth."

I smiled. "Just spreading some sweetness and light, Dooley."

"Well, I sure didn't know cat litter is good for almost anything."

"It certainly is, my friend. Maybe cat litter is the panacea we've all been looking for. Maybe it can even cure cancer and bring about world peace."

"Now you're pulling my paw, aren't you, Max?"

"Maybe just a little," I confessed.

But as we watched our humans hug and be happy, I thought that maybe, just maybe, cat litter could do all that and more. After all, cats were created to make the world a better place. So why wouldn't our litter serve the same purpose?

It certainly made me happy every time I felt that pleasant texture under my paws when I did my business. And I know that my friends all felt the same way. But since we'd had a very stressful couple of days, finally my eyes drooped closed, and moments later I was asleep... almost.

"Max?"

"Mh?"

"Can cat litter really cure cancer?"

"I wouldn't be surprised if it did."

"So... do you have to ingest it?"

"Something like that." But then, since I was fairly sure that Dooley would go ahead and do exactly that, I quickly amended my statement. "Please don't eat cat litter, Dooley."

"I won't, Max," he said. "This time *I* was pulling *your* paw."

"Oh, good. Cause if you did swallow it, things would probably get blocked... down there."

"Which would be a good thing, since you wouldn't need to go to the litter box anymore. Which would save our humans money. And cure all of our diseases."

I eyed him closely but could see no signs of deception. "Dooley, please don't—"

"I'm just kidding, Max! I'm trying to become as good a liar as you. Is it working, do you think?"

"It's working," I admitted.

"I'll feed some cat litter to Grace. That way, she can get rid of her diapers. And I'll feed some of it to Gran, as she's always complaining of creaky knees. And to Uncle Alec, to fill up his stomach so he can keep dieting. And to—"

Oh, dear. Looked like I had created a litter monster!

THE END

Thanks for reading! If you want to know when a new Nic Saint book comes out, sign up for Nic's mailing list: nicsaint.com/news

EXCERPT FROM PURRFECT GHOST (MAX 71)

Chapter One

Holly Mitchell checked the big chest of toys in the living room for a sign of her daughter's security blanket. Ruby, who was four, had been crying up a storm all day, wondering where her precious rabbit-shaped blankie could be. She had probably dropped it somewhere, or possibly their teacup Chihuahua Babette had taken the blanket and buried it out in the backyard. But wherever it was, she better find it. Ruby's big brother Sylvester had been trying to comfort his little sister, but to no avail. Without Mr. Longears she simply would not be comforted.

"Here, give her this," said Holly's mom, and surreptitiously handed Holly a blankie that looked almost indistinguishable from the original. "I got it from the same store," she added under her breath. The four of them had gone to the mall that evening, and had just now arrived home.

"I guess it's worth a shot," Holly said, and proceeded to make a big display of 'discovering' Mr. Longears under one of the couch cushions. "Ooh, look who I found!" she cried.

Ruby's face lit up like a Christmas tree, but as she grabbed for her precious toy, she said, "He smells funny!"

"That's because I washed him," Holly explained. "Even rabbits need a bath sometimes."

Ruby gazed up at her with those big eyes of hers, then smiled a gummy smile and proceeded to bury her face into her blankie. "I missed you, Mr. Longears!" she declared solemnly. "Don't run away again!"

"Mission accomplished," Holly told her mom with satisfaction. The mystery of the missing blankie hadn't been solved, but at least Ruby was happy again, and that was all that mattered.

It wasn't always easy to raise two kids on her own, but fortunately she got a lot of help from her mom and dad. After her husband Eric had died in a freak accident four years ago, she suddenly found herself a widow, and the adjustment, coming on top of the grief of Eric's death, had been painful. But somehow they had all managed to find a new normal and adjust as well as they could. Even though the kids still asked about their daddy from time to time, especially Sylvester, who had been four at the time, they didn't seem to have been adversely affected too much. They both did well in school, and Holly tried to make their home as warm and cozy and happy as she could.

"I don't think you should go," her mom now said.

"Why? Can't you babysit them?" she asked.

"No, it's not that. It's just that…" Mom made an ineffectual gesture with her hand. "I don't know. Maybe this is just me being silly, but I've just got a bad feeling about this, you know. Especially since…" She glanced over to where the kids were sitting on the couch, both admiring Mr. Longears.

"It's not going to happen again, Mom," Holly assured her. "Freak accidents are exactly that: freakish in their rarity. It's not going to happen again," she repeated, more to herself than to her mom. It was true that the same thought had entered her mind when her boss had selected her to give a sales presentation to their Boston team. Eric, too, had been on his way to an important presentation when his car suddenly veered off the road and had crashed into a ditch. No other drivers had been on the road that night, and the brakes on his car had functioned perfectly. The insurance company and the police had conducted their investigations, but neither had been able to explain what caused Eric's car to careen off the road like that. And now she would be heading to the same hotel in the same city to give a presentation. If her boss had known about what happened to her husband, maybe he wouldn't have selected her. But then she wasn't the kind of person who liked to discuss her private affairs.

"Okay, so maybe you can tell them that now is not a good time," her mom suggested. "That you need to be with your family right now? Maybe tell them that Ruby is, I don't know, teething?"

Which wasn't a lie, since the last of Ruby's baby teeth had recently started appearing. In that sense she was definitely a latecomer, but according to the dentist it was nothing to worry about.

"If I did that, they'd simply select someone else to give the presentation, Mom."

"So? Is that so bad?"

"It would also put me down a few pegs in the pecking order. Next time a big presentation comes up, they'll think twice about asking me. And before you know it, I'll be gently pushed toward the exit."

"That's a pretty inhumane way to run a company."

"Inhumane or not, they want to know they can always rely on me."

"It's the anniversary of Eric's…" She glanced over to the kids, then whispered, "Well, you know."

"Of course I know, Mom. But if I let Eric's death control my life like that, I'll never go anywhere ever again. Accidents happen, and just because it happened to Eric doesn't mean it will happen to me."

"Maybe you could ask someone to drive you," Mom mused. "Book an Uber, maybe?"

"It's fine. I'll be careful," she promised.

"And call me every hour on the hour to let me know how you're doing." She frowned. "Or maybe we should turn it into a family trip? We could all join you. The kids, me, your dad. You know, we could see the city while you do whatever it is that you have to do, and then we'll meet up at the hotel and have a good time. That way I won't spend the whole weekend worrying about you."

She smiled at her mom. "That's sweet of you, Mom, but it's really not necessary. I'll be all right."

"Who's talking about you? I'll be worried sick, and I'm not even talking about your dad. With his heart condition, he shouldn't be put through the wringer like this."

Holly thought about this. Her mom was right, of course. It was bad enough that Dad had lost his beloved son-in-law. If he ever lost his daughter too, that would be the end of him. But then she knew she couldn't think like that, or she would never venture out of the house again—ever. So instead, she decided to change the topic. "So have you and Dad decided on the big move yet?"

Mom made a throwaway gesture with her hand. "Oh, forget about that. Your dad will never go along with me on that one. If I didn't know any better, I'd say he wants to keep on living in that house forever—until his dying day. I keep telling him that place is much too big for us, and we should sell and move into something smaller. But you know your dad. The man is as stubborn as a mule. He keeps telling me that when you repot a plant there's a good chance that it will die. And so if we repot ourselves, there's always a chance we won't survive."

"People aren't plants, Mom," she pointed out.

"I know that, and you know that, but try telling that to your dad!"

"Anyway, sooner or later you'll have to move. That garden doesn't take care of itself, and neither does the house."

Mom and Dad had bought the big house anticipating they'd raise a big family. And they had. With five kids in the house, at one time it had seemed too small to accommodate them all, especially when they had hit their teens and needed a lot of personal space. But since they had all left, the house definitely was too big to maintain, and even though they had been gently pushing their dad to sell up and move into a comfortable apartment in town, with an elevator and all the comforts he and Mom needed, the man was refusing to budge.

"Until he finally sees the light," said Mom, "I'll have to keep paying Maria to come in twice a week, and Arturio to keep up gardening duties. At least those two are very happy with your dad's stubbornness."

To Holly and her siblings their parents' marriage was the gold standard by which they measured their own relationships. Even after forty years the love and respect they had for each other was still palpable. According to Mom it hadn't always been that way, and shortly after they were married they had hit a rough patch. But as she liked to tell the story they had worked to overcome their differences, and after having raised five kids who now all had kids of their own, their marriage was stronger than ever. Now if only Dad would let go of the old house. Holly understood, though, and secretly didn't want them to sell the place either. After all, there were so many memories there—all happy ones.

Holly and her mother watched for a moment as the kids sat transfixed by the new and improved Mr. Longears, with Ruby giving him a million kisses and Sylvester giving his sister a big protecting cuddle. Then Holly went in search of Babette, who had been barking up a storm in the kitchen. She had almost reached the back door, assuming Babette wanted to be let out of the house—they always locked the pet door when they went out—when she almost stumbled over something lying on the floor. She switched on the light and, as she took a closer look, discovered to her horror that it was a man she had never seen before. And if she wasn't mistaken, the man was very much dead!

Chapter Two

Mark Cooper watched the hullabaloo going on across the street from his bedroom window. There were a lot of lights flashing and police cars coming and going, and he wondered what was going on. As a retired math teacher, he knew the odds of a tragic event taking place in the same family were slim to none, so a second death taking place in the same family was highly unlikely. Probably the mother had taken a bad fall and had to be taken to the hospital, he thought. Or maybe the dad had suffered a cardiac arrest. He hoped the kids were all right. Even though he didn't like Holly, he wouldn't want to see any harm come to her kids. After all, they couldn't help it if their mom was an annoying so-and-so.

The family had definitely suffered through their share of tragedy, with Eric Mitchell dying a couple of years ago. Though this idea that Holly and Eric had been a dream couple was nonsense, of course. Once he'd passed by their house late at night walking Melvin, and he'd heard the couple engaged in a screaming match that had turned his ears red and had even caused Melvin to look up in alarm. Young love, he thought at the time. One minute they're crazy about each other, and the next they can drink each other's blood.

According to the scuttlebutt, Eric had died in a road accident. Driven his car into a ditch. Holly had turned from a blushing young bride into a widow overnight, and now, four years on, there was still no sign of a new man in her life. Maybe there would never be one. Some women were like that. They lost the love of their lives and never wanted to remarry again. To be honest, he had also been like that. But then he and Jackie had been together fifty-five years before she passed, which was more than Holly and Eric ever had.

Next to him, Melvin also looked at the house across the street, fascinated by all the bright lights.

"What do you say if we take our walk now, Melvin?" he suggested. He could linger across the road for a while, joining the other rubberneckers and ambulance chasers, and maybe find out what was going on over there. He'd read all about it in tomorrow's paper, of course, or on the *Gazette* website. For he'd already seen that Odelia Kingsley woman arrive, along with her husband Chase, the police detective. As usual, they were accompanied by their cats, which struck him as very strange indeed, but then such was life in Hampton Cove. All the eccentrics seemed to flock there. "Must be something in the water," he told Melvin. And as if he understood what his human was saying, the poodle yapped in agreement.

* * *

Mae West was just on her way back from the dog park, where she had walked her Alsatian, Roger Moore, when she was struck by the presence of all those police cars on her street. When she drew closer, she saw that they had all gathered at the place where the Mitchells lived, though it was probably more accurate to say that Holly Mitchell lived there, since Eric had died a couple of years ago now, in some tragic accident she didn't know the details about, nor did anyone else as far as she knew.

"Now what do we have here?" she asked as she approached. The police had cordoned off the area, so she couldn't actually get close to where the action was, and she joined the other people gawking at the events as they unfolded. She found herself standing next to Mark Cooper. Mark had come out accompanied by his poodle, Melvin, and as the two dogs proceeded to sniff at each other, she and Mark exchanged a greeting. Even though she had never particularly liked Mark, she had always tried to maintain a cordial relationship with the man, if only because they were neighbors and forced to bump into each other on a regular basis, especially since they were both dog owners and met one another in the local dog park every day. All the dog owners on the block were members of the same WhatsApp group and kept in touch that way. But Mark, being one of the more overbearing neighbors she had ever encountered, liked to boss the others around to some extent, something she hated.

Her husband, Julio, had always said about Mark that if he had been a general in the army, his own soldiers would have turned against him and shot him. But since they were merely neighbors and Mark wasn't a general but a retired math teacher, no shootings had occurred so far.

"What's going on?" she asked.

"No idea," said Mark. "It started about an hour ago. First,

one police car arrived, then an ambulance, then this whole fleet of police cars. That Kingsley reporter went in with her detective husband, so it must be something big if those two are involved."

Mae knew just what Mark was referring to. Chase Kingsley and his wife were big on handling murder inquiries, of which there had been far too many recently. So if they had gone in, this couldn't be Holly's mom who had stumbled over the dog and taken a nasty tumble.

"Do you think... It's murder?" she asked.

"Has to be," said Mark, "if the Kingsleys are involved. And the Kingsley woman had her cats along with her, so that probably means they'll be here all night, sniffing out clues and generally making a big spectacle of things." He sniffed audibly, and contempt was written all over his features. Not every dog owner hates cats, but Mark sure did. In fact, it wasn't too much to say he abhorred the species with a vengeance and wouldn't have minded if cats became extinct at some point.

"I can't imagine. Murder? Here on our street? But who? And why?"

"Like I said, no idea," Mark confessed, and he sounded disappointed as he said it.

"You don't think... Holly?" asked Mae. Even though she wasn't overly fond of Holly Mitchell, she couldn't help but feel some measure of sympathy for the woman. After the tragedy that had befallen her, she still did her best to give those kids of hers a good upbringing. Her parents had been a big help, of course, especially Holly's mom, who was always there to take care of her grandkids.

"I think it must be the mother," Mark now said. "Maybe they got into a fight and things got out of hand. I just can't see what else it could be," he hastened to add when Mae expressed her shock and dismay at these words.

"I just can't believe it," she said. "I only hope... It's not one of those family tragedies you always hear about. You know, that she first killed her kids and then herself."

Mark's face contorted into a frown. "I hope you're right," he said. "Now that would be a tragedy."

She glanced up at her neighbor. Rumor had it that Mark Cooper had been sweet on Holly for a while. Though he was far too old for the woman, of course. But it had to be said that Holly Mitchell was an attractive woman. Possibly too attractive for a widow. But then she had become a widow at a very young age. They had only been married a few short years when tragedy struck.

Roger Moore was straining at the leash to take a look, and now she saw what had caused him to become restless. The Kingsleys were walking out of the house, accompanied by their cats. Roger Moore barked at the cats, and so did Melvin. The cats looked a little intimidated, she thought. They were a big red cat and a small fluffy beige-gray one. Odd, she thought, that the Kingsley woman wouldn't go anywhere without her cats in tow. Then again, she never went anywhere without Roger Moore, so maybe it wasn't all that odd. Just that people didn't usually take their cats with them. They might be companion animals, but not when you ventured out of the home.

One of their neighbors shouted a question at the passing detective, but Kingsley merely held up his hand. No comment, the gesture seemed to suggest.

"Who died?" she suddenly found herself piping up. But the couple passed by without deigning her with a response. Looked like they'd have to read about it in the paper or see it on their local news. And since Roger Moore had started tugging on his leash, eager to get home and have a bite to eat, she said goodbye to Mark and headed on home. On the way there, she passed Norma Parkman, the butcher's wife, and wondered what the woman had done to her face this time.

* * *

Norma Parkman wondered why that Mae West woman was staring at her as if she had something stuck to her face. But then she was used to being gawked at on a regular basis. Most people she met seemed to find her fascinating to look at, and so over the years, she had begun to consider it a compliment. Her husband Mikel always said it was because she didn't look like most people, and so they had to adjust their expectations when they first met her. He said she was exotic and had an interesting face. She knew this to be all too true, for when she looked in the mirror in the morning, she sometimes had to adjust her own expectations too. Then again, it was a tough struggle trying to remain as youthful-looking as she did. Oddly enough, it only seemed to become more difficult as the years passed. At fifty-seven, she some-times felt she was fighting a losing battle, but then Mikel said that was nonsense and she looked every bit as lovely as she had when they first met, back when they were both fresh-faced eighteen-year-olds.

She gave Mike's leash a light yank and wondered why it was always her who had to take the damn pug for a walk and why Mikel was inside watching television while she was out there being bored to tears while Mike took his sweet time to do his business. When she caught sight of the flashing lights and the array of police vehicles parked in front of the Mitchell place, her first thought was that Holly's dad had had another stroke. After that first one he'd had a couple of years ago, it was only a matter of time before he suffered a second one, more debilitating this time and possibly deadly. It was always the way, wasn't it?

She just hoped he hadn't died. Holly had already had her share of heartache over the years. First Eric had died, and then, as a consequence, Eric's own dad had suffered cardiac arrest and had turned into a vegetable, only to die six months to the day his son had died. And then Eric's grief-stricken mother had also died, wilting like a flower, as one of their neighbors had described it. She was a nurse in the hospital where both Eric's parents had been admitted and said it was as clear a death from grief as she had ever seen.

So now Holly only had her own mom and dad left, and if the good Lord took those away as well, that would be terrible.

Oh, life just wasn't fair sometimes, was it? Just look at her. Her last boob job had been botched by that terrible surgeon, and now her left boob was slightly bigger than her right, and not only that, but it hung lower than its cousin. Mikel said he didn't mind, but she sure as heck did. She had already made another appointment at the clinic, but if she had to go under the knife again, it would be her fifth boob job in as many years, and frankly, she was starting to wonder when this would end. And then the girl who'd done her Botox this time must have been asleep on the job, for she had ended up with excruciating pain in her left eye and an eyelid that had refused to remain in place. Almost as if the girl had hit a nerve or something. It was a ghastly sight, and for a whole three days, she had been nervous about waiting on people in the butcher shop, afraid they'd start making comments again behind her back as she knew they always did.

She joined the group of neighbors looking at the scene, and when she saw Chris Goldsworthy, she tiptoed up to him. Chris always knew what was going on in their neighborhood. The man was a veritable fountain of wisdom. Chairman of their local watch committee, he made it his business to be informed. It didn't hurt that he was also drop-dead-gorgeous handsome. He reminded her of Don Johnson, who she always thought aged very well. "What's going on, Chris?" she asked. "Who died?"

"I'm not sure," said Chris, much to her surprise. "I think it must be serious, though, I just saw that detective come and go. Chase Kingsley? And also, the county coroner was in there. Abe Cornwall. So if they were here, it can't just be a heart attack or some accident—someone falling from the stairs or cutting themselves with the kitchen knife." He shook his head decidedly. "I think this just might be..."

She stared at him with a mixture of anticipation and dread. "What?"

He turned to her and lowered his voice. "Murder," he said, and she had the impression he actually took relish in the ghoulish fact.

She shivered. "Murder? But how can that be?"

"Murder happens everywhere, Nonnie," he said, using his favorite name for her, though he always made sure that Mikel didn't hear it, since he would only get jealous. That was the problem with Chris: all women adored him, and all men hated him, exactly because of that fact. "Even on our street."

"Maybe some burglary gone wrong," she suggested, for she simply couldn't imagine one member of Holly's family murdering another member. Holly herself was always so distinguished, so kind and unruffled, in spite of the tragedies that had befallen her. And Holly's mom was just the same. Nice, well-respected people, Charlie and Bethany Williams.

"You're probably right," Chris agreed. "Maybe they caught a burglar, and there was a struggle, and in the process, someone died."

Norma stared intently at the house, hoping to catch sight of either Holly, the kids, or her parents. But nothing. Absolutely nothing.

"I better run on home," she announced.

Chris's lips morphed into a smirk. "To tell Mikel what's going on?"

"Of course not," she said, even though he had guessed right. Whenever she had big news to impart, she couldn't wait to get home and tell her husband. He loved all the gossip from the neighborhood, and she loved supplying it to him. And this was certainly the most exciting gossip they'd had in ages. Not since old Mrs. Rutherford had fallen out with her long-time friend Mrs. Davis, and the two old ladies had engaged in a shouting match that had quickly turned physical, did they have the kind of news that earned the qualification 'shocking.'

She just wished she could ascertain who had died. Now that would be a scoop! But if even Chris Goldsworthy didn't know, she certainly wasn't going to find out any time soon. Unless...

She took out her phone and opened her WhatsApp app to check the dog walkers' group.

"Checking the dog walkers' scuttlebutt?" asked Chris with amusement.

She nodded. Though if Chris didn't know what was going on, chances were the other members of the WhatsApp group wouldn't know either, since he was one of the group's most active members.

"And? Any luck?" he asked.

"Nothing," she said sadly. "Even Mark Cooper doesn't seem to know what's going on, and he lives right across the street."

They both glanced behind them at the Cooper place. The lights were on, but of Mark, there was no trace.

"Too bad," said Chris with a sigh. "I probably won't be able to sleep until I know exactly what's going on. You?"

"Yeah, I'm the same way," she admitted. "Stuff like this keeps me up at night."

"But not Mikel, right?"

"No, not Mikel," she admitted with a smile. Mikel was an excellent sleeper. Her husband fell asleep the moment his head hit the pillow, while she could be tossing and turning all night. Or she would finally nod off, only to be wide awake at three, not able to go back to sleep. It was very annoying, especially since they both had to get up early to open the store. But then that couldn't be helped.

"That's because he's a man with a clear conscience," Chris declared, and it could be her imagination, but he seemed to be looking at her just that little bit more intently as he said it.

"I better run," she said. Mikel had sent her a message, she saw, asking her what was taking her so long. He was the best husband in the world, bar none, but he had the annoying habit of being very jealous. Even if a guy looked at her funnily in the store or paid her a compliment, Mikel could get worked up. Good thing he had the good sense never to act on his emotions, especially with the customers, or they could have kissed their business goodbye a long time ago. But even though he rarely said anything, knowing how much it annoyed her, she could feel it when the temperature in their otherwise cozy living room would drop to zero, and he'd sulk and mope all evening before suddenly doing a full about-face and becoming sweet like a pussy cat, showering her with kisses.

One of those psychological quirks, according to a survey in Cosmo she had once read. When you marry a guy, you take the good with the bad, and after all these years, she knew that every guy came with a flaw of some kind. Even Chris Goldsworthy, the most perfect man she had ever met.

But oh boy, did he come with a major flaw!

Chapter Three

It isn't often that Dooley and I have to postpone our trip to join cat choir because some tragedy happened elsewhere. Mostly, murderers like to stick to business hours and make sure we don't have to interrupt our regular schedule to mop up the unfortunate aftermath of their nefarious activities. But today was different. Odelia and Chase had already settled in for the evening and were watching some instructive program on television—*Project Runway* if I'm not mistaken—and Grace had retired to bed for the night, while Dooley and I were just about to step out and join our friends in the park to practice our singing voices when the call came in.

Chase was the one to pick up since he's the designated cop in our pleasant little household. From his demeanor I could tell that something not all that pleasant had taken place. Normally, when in a resting state, Chase is mostly easygoing, warm-hearted, one might even say fun to be around. But when he turns his mind to murder and mayhem, which basically is what his profession revolves around, his brows knit together in a frown, the corners of his lips turn down, and generally, he behaves as if there's been a shooting somewhere, which more often than not there has been.

As it turned out a shooting had, in fact, taken place, and our urgent attention was required.

The body had been found by one Holly Mitchell, who happened to live on Russell Street, which is right around the corner from Harrington Street, where we live.

As we walked over there to ascertain how truthful Mrs. Mitchell's 911 call actually was, Chase gave us some more information to go on. "Body of an unknown male discovered by homeowner Holly Mitchell. Mrs. Mitchell lives alone in the house with her two kids and had her mother over for a visit, something that happens very frequently, when she decided to go into the kitchen to let the dog out. That's when she practically stumbled over the body of this man she had never seen before."

"Could be a vagrant who decided to try his luck through the back door," Odelia suggested.

"Could be," Chase agreed in a noncommittal way that is common with him. As long as he hasn't taken in the scene with his own two eyes and ascertained what could have happened, he's reluctant to commit himself to this explanation or that, or generally put the cart before the horse, so to speak.

In due course we arrived at the address indicated and saw that we weren't exactly the first to arrive. Quite the contrary, in fact, as the coroner was there, an ambulance, but also several police vehicles, with officers cordoning off the area and making sure nobody could pass through and take a look at the unfortunate victim.

We walked into the house, having to hurry up since Chase has very long legs and Odelia is pretty quick off the mark as well, and traversed a cozy-looking living room where an older lady sat on the couch with two kids, accompanied by a younger woman who did not look happy to see us. This was probably Holly Mitchell, the person who had stumbled across the dead man, her mother and two kids.

Odelia and Chase introduced themselves to the woman, who was indeed the lady of the manor, and then we proceeded into the kitchen. The victim still lay where Mrs. Mitchell had found him, and for a few moments, Odelia and Chase studied the body from every angle before finally reaching the conclusion that, "The man is dead." This from Chase, who is a professional at this kind of thing.

"Yeah, looks like it," Odelia agreed, also a professional.

And because all good things come in threes, Abe Cornwall, the county coroner, added his own two cents to the conversation by stating, "He's dead, all right."

"I think the man is dead, Max," Dooley said.

"Yes, we've established that," I said.

We moved closer to the body, and immediately I was struck by the strong body odor the man emitted, and also the terrible state of his clothes, an old pair of stained jeans and an equally stained sweater. Almost as if he had lived on the street for a long time and hadn't seen a shower in a while.

Abe pointed to a crimson spot on the man's chest. "Shot through the heart," he announced. "Twenty-two-caliber gun, most likely. The body was still warm when I got here, so I'd say he died between one and two hours ago."

"How many shots?" asked Chase, who looked all business as he studied the dead man, who was lying on his back.

"One bullet, as far as I can tell," said Abe. "Though I'll send you my report later, once I know more about what happened here."

"I think it's obvious what happened," said Odelia. "Mrs. Mitchell caught this man breaking into her house, and so she shot him. But then she realized she might be in serious trouble, so she decided not to mention the break-in or the shooting and claim she had nothing to do with the man's death at all."

"There's no gun registered in Holly Mitchell's name," said Chase, checking something on his phone.

"That doesn't mean anything," Odelia pointed out. She had crouched down next to the victim. "Any ID?"

"Nothing," said Abe. "So we'll have to find out who he is some other way."

"Mrs. Mitchell claims she's never seen the man before," said a police officer, likely the person who had arrived first on the scene. "She says she walked into her kitchen to let the dog out and almost stumbled over the man."

Odelia shot us a meaningful look, and I knew just what that look meant: talk to the dog! And so we went in search of the dog to interview the creature.

We found the dog in the living room, where it sat huddled on the couch, snug and safe behind its human. As far as I could tell, it was a teacup Chihuahua, which is like a regular Chihuahua, only a lot smaller. The dog didn't seem happy to see us as it burrowed even deeper into the couch when we approached.

"What are these cats doing here?" asked the dog's owner, giving us a curious look, as if she had never seen a cat before in her life. Then again, we often get that look, as people don't usually expect a police officer to be accompanied by two cats. But then Odelia isn't a police officer but a police consultant, and we're not regular cats but Odelia's consultants. So you could say that we're a consultant's consultants and have every right to be present at the crime scene, no matter how odd people will look at us.

"Hi there," I said to the little doggie. But instead of replying, the dog merely stared at us, its tongue sticking out between its lips, giving it a funny look.

"My name is Dooley, and this is Max," said Dooley helpfully. "What is your name?"

But the dog either wasn't aware of its own name, or it wasn't talking. So Dooley and I decided to move into the second play in our playbook. It's something we've picked up from Chase himself.

"You did this, didn't you!" I said, adopting a harsh tone of voice. "You killed that man!"

"Oh, don't listen to my friend," said Dooley. "He's just a little cranky because he hasn't eaten."

"I'm cranky because I hate it when dogs misbehave!" I shouted.

"It's all right," said Dooley. "You can misbehave all you

want, Mr. Dog, or is it Mrs. Dog? Or possibly even Miss Dog? I mean, it's your home, you can do whatever you want in here, even murder a trespasser. Because that's what happened, right? This man trespassed, and you killed him?"

"But I didn't kill anyone!" said the dog, proving once again that the good cat, bad cat routine never fails to bring the required result. "He was lying there on the floor, dead, when I first laid eyes on him."

"And who made him that way?" asked Dooley.

"I have no idea!" said the doggie, whimpering slightly and quivering from stem to stern. "You have to believe me, good sirs. I would never cause harm to anyone. I've never even bitten a person in my life."

"You've never bitten anyone?" I asked with a touch of gruffness. "A likely story! Now talk, dog, 'cause you're in a heap of trouble here!"

"What's your name?" asked Dooley.

"Babette," said the dog, eyeing me as if I was the worst cat in history, which maybe I was at that moment. Though I have to say, it felt strangely exhilarating to unleash my inner monster for once. "And I honestly don't know what happened, sirs."

"You've never seen this man before?" asked Dooley in kindly tones.

"Never!" Babette said. "I swear. He's certainly not from around here since all the people on the block have dogs, and they walk them every day, so I know all our neighbors, and this guy was never here."

"You walk every day?" asked Dooley. "Isn't that bad for those short legs of yours?"

"Oh, but I love walking," said the dog fervently. "It's my favorite time of the day when my mistress decides to take me out of the house, and we go down to the dog park. I get to hang out with the other dogs while our humans all shoot the breeze. It's great fun."

"Odd that we've never met," I said. "We hang out at the dog park from time to time."

The doggie's eyes went even wider now. "If we had met, I would definitely remember, Mr. Max. I could never forget a cat like you!"

I had a feeling I'd done my work a little too well and had put the fear of God into this dog. So I now relaxed. "I'm sorry for scaring you," I said. "But like my friend Dooley says, I haven't eaten, and when I'm hungry, I tend to get cranky."

The dog's face broke into a huge smile. "Oh, but I can totally relate. When I don't eat, I also get cranky. Very cranky indeed!"

"You wouldn't... happen to have some leftovers for us, would you?" asked Dooley. "It's just that all this murder business always makes me hungry."

"Me too," I admitted.

"Follow me!" said the dog, having become animated now that she realized we weren't going to bring out the handcuffs and place her under arrest. So we followed her into the kitchen, and she led us straight to her bowl, which contained some delicious-smelling kibble. But before we could dig in, Odelia actually swooped in, scooped up the bowl, and placed it on the kitchen counter!

"Hey!" I said, still holding on to my alternate persona, which I tentatively would have called 'Mad Max.' "What do you think you're doing? We were going to eat that!"

"No, you're not," said Odelia decidedly. "We're guests here, Max, and guests don't go around eating food from their host without first receiving an invitation."

"But she did offer us an invitation," I said, pointing to Babette.

Odelia smiled. "The owner needs to offer an invitation," she clarified, "not the owner's dog."

"A new rule," said Dooley with a touch of sadness. "Always new rules to follow, Max. It does get complicated after a while, doesn't it?"

"It sure does," I said with a sigh.

"Just dig in!" Babette whispered invitingly. "I'll cover for you!"

"Cover for us?" I asked with a frown. But since Babette clearly believed in giving service, she now suddenly jumped up, dug her teeth into Chase's calf, and didn't let go again. It was a funny sight: the dog hung from Chase's leg, her tiny teeth just sharp enough to provide some traction against his jeans but not sharp enough to cut through the fabric and into Chase's actual leg and do damage.

The cop lifted his leg and studied the dangling dog for a moment, then smiled. "Aren't you just the cutest, sweetest little dog?"

I could tell that Babette wanted to respond to this, but since that meant she had to let go of her quarry, she decided to give the cop the silent treatment instead.

Unfortunately she was no match for the cop, so he simply plucked her from his leg like one plucks an apple from a tree and held her in the palm of his hand. "And what's your name, huh?" he said. "Isn't he just the cutest, babe?"

"He is," Odelia confirmed as she tickled the doggie behind the ears.

"Now, Mr. Max!" said Babette. "They're distracted!"

Normally, I'm not all that quick off the mark, but I was feeling peckish, so I didn't need to be told twice. And while our humans enjoyed themselves with Babette, Dooley and I quickly nabbed the few remaining nuggets of kibble from her bowl. They certainly hit the spot.

"Thanks, Babette," I said.

"Don't mention it," said the doggie.

But when Odelia looked back and saw the empty bowl, her expression clouded. And I had the impression she would have said something, but at that moment, Abe walked back in, accompanied by one of his assistants, so she merely proceeded to glower at us.

Somehow, I had a feeling she wasn't happy with our work. But at least my stomach wasn't empty anymore, so we could get on with the case. I mean, it's hard to detect and hunt for clues on an empty stomach! Even detectives have to eat.

ABOUT NIC

Nic has a background in political science and before being struck by the writing bug worked odd jobs around the world (including but not limited to massage therapist in Mexico, gardener in Italy, restaurant manager in India, and Berlitz teacher in Belgium).

When he's not writing he enjoys curling up with a good (comic) book, watching British crime dramas, French comedies or Nancy Meyers movies, sampling pastry (apple cake!), pasta and chocolate (preferably the dark variety), twisting himself into a pretzel doing morning yoga, going for a run, and spoiling his big red tomcat Tommy.

He lives with his wife (and aforementioned cat) in a small village smack dab in the middle of absolutely nowhere and is probably writing his next 'Mysteries of Max' book right now.

www.nicsaint.com

ALSO BY NIC SAINT

The Mysteries of Max

Purrfect Murder

Purrfectly Deadly

Purrfect Revenge

Purrfect Heat

Purrfect Crime

Purrfect Rivalry

Purrfect Peril

Purrfect Secret

Purrfect Alibi

Purrfect Obsession

Purrfect Betrayal

Purrfectly Clueless

Purrfectly Royal

Purrfect Cut

Purrfect Trap

Purrfectly Hidden

Purrfect Kill

Purrfect Boy Toy

Purrfectly Dogged

Purrfectly Dead

Purrfect Saint

Purrfect Advice

Purrfect Passion

A Purrfect Gnomeful

Purrfect Cover

Purrfect Patsy

Purrfect Son

Purrfect Fool

Purrfect Fitness

Purrfect Setup

Purrfect Sidekick

Purrfect Deceit

Purrfect Ruse

Purrfect Swing

Purrfect Cruise

Purrfect Harmony

Purrfect Sparkle

Purrfect Cure

Purrfect Cheat

Purrfect Catch

Purrfect Design

Purrfect Life

Purrfect Thief

Purrfect Crust

Purrfect Bachelor

Purrfect Double

Purrfect Date

Purrfect Hit

Purrfect Baby

Purrfect Mess

Purrfect Paris

Purrfect Model

Purrfect Slug

Purrfect Match

Purrfect Game

Purrfect Bouquet

Purrfect Home

Purrfectly Slim

Purrfect Nap

Purrfect Yacht

Purrfect Scam

Purrfect Fury

Purrfect Christmas

Purrfect Gems

Purrfect Demons

Purrfect Show

Purrfect Impasse

Purrfect Charade

Purrfect Zoo

Purrfect Star

The Mysteries of Max Collections

Murder at the Art Class

Washington & Jefferson

First Shot

Alice Whitehouse

Spooky Times

Spooky Trills

Spooky End

Spooky Spells

Ghosts of London

Between a Ghost and a Spooky Place

Public Ghost Number One

Ghost Save the Queen

Box Set 1 (Books 1-3)

A Tale of Two Harrys

Ghost of Girlband Past

Ghostlier Things

Charleneland

Deadly Ride

Final Ride

Neighborhood Witch Committee

Witchy Start

Witchy Worries

Witchy Wishes

Saffron Diffley

Crime and Retribution

Vice and Verdict

Felonies and Penalties (Saffron Diffley Short 1)

The B-Team

Once Upon a Spy

Tate-à-Tate

Enemy of the Tates

Ghosts vs. Spies

The Ghost Who Came in from the Cold

Witchy Fingers

Witchy Trouble

Witchy Hexations

Witchy Possessions

Witchy Riches

Box Set 1 (Books 1-4)

The Mysteries of Bell & Whitehouse

One Spoonful of Trouble

Two Scoops of Murder

Three Shots of Disaster

Box Set 1 (Books 1-3)

A Twist of Wraith

A Touch of Ghost

A Clash of Spooks

Box Set 2 (Books 4-6)

The Stuffing of Nightmares

A Breath of Dead Air

An Act of Hodd

Box Set 3 (Books 7-9)

A Game of Dons

Standalone Novels

When in Bruges

The Whiskered Spy

ThrillFix

Homejacking

The Eighth Billionaire

The Wrong Woman

Printed in Great Britain
by Amazon

26999736R00138